DAVID C. MARTIN

CHARLESTOWN

Charlestown
Copyright © 2024 by David C. Martin

Library of Congress Control Number: 2024914211

ISBN
978-1-964982-03-8 (Paperback)
978-1-964982-04-5 (eBook)

Table of Contents

I 1
II.. 5
III 18
IV 24
V.. 30
VI 35
VII 41
VIII.. 50
IX 56
X.. 59
XI 65
XII 71
XIII.. 74
XIV.. 84
XV 87
XVI.. 99
XVII 103

It is 7:00 A.M, Boston Time

Another in a series of cold, drizzly, overcast Saturdays, beginning around Labor Day, here in Boston. It's wicked frigid, but at least it's Saturday.

Upstairs, Benjamin Blumberg rents this particular top-floor walk-up on High Street, in a triple-decker, thought to have been inhabited at one time by Civil War turn-coat Albert Gallatin Blanchard, in Charlestown. In this Revolutionary town, any Civil history is especially rare.

Albert was born here in antebellum Charlestown, when it was still an independent city, prior to annexation into sprawling Boston, and was educated at West Point, along with classmate Robert E. Lee. When he fell in love with and married Marie Louise Herminie Benoist of New Orleans, he found himself on the wrong side of history, at the wrong time.

He served admirably in the Mexican War, but upon the outbreak of hostilities between the States, Albert entered the 1st Louisiana Infantry, rising to rank of Brigadier General, and prior to retiring, helped unsuccessfully defend Augusta against Sherman's March to the Sea. General Blanchard is buried in The Big Easy, one of the very few Bostonians to have achieved high rank fighting against the Union forces in the War Between the States.

From Albert and Ben's rear porch, one can look South to the Tobin Bridge and across to the city of Cambridge.

Benjamin has been a proud Boston cabbie for thirteen years. But today will not be his lucky day.

His girlfriend, Amy Adams, has been with Benjamin for three years now. Amy is an attractive and tall, well-postured and lightly-freckled redhead, with straight shiny hair extending to below her shoulder blades. Amy is a graduate student, and a researcher at the Boston Public Library, working on determining the authenticity of 18th-Century letters within the collection. While Amy is devoted to Benjamin, she is content as his girlfriend.

But today is Saint Patrick's Day. It is a holiday of the highest degree in Boston. Amy is up early and bubbling away in the Jacuzzi. She is looking forward to the Saint Patrick's Day parade and the daylong celebration of corned beef, cabbage, alcohol consumption and good cheer that is the tradition for Saint Patrick's Day.

Unfortunately, Amy never does get to the celebration.

Benjamin is still in bed. He had a difficult Friday night shift that ended at 12:00 midnight. On the way home, he stopped at the Morning Glory Bar on Salem Street for a pre-Saint Patrick's Day warm-up of boilermakers. At 2:00 A.M., Mick the bartender yelled, "bottoms up boys, I'm going home."

Barry obliged with a last shot of Jameson Irish Whisky, and then found his way home to sleep it off.

Less than five hours later, his cell phone on the nightstand starts to ring. Groggily, Benjamin answers the phone. "Hello".

"Where the hell are you? The client is landing in Cambridge in five minutes," the loud voice continues, "he expects his ride to be here, waiting for him."

Benjamin had agreed to provide chauffer services for a out-of-town union official today. The official is Harry Sharpstone, an organizer for the Teamsters. He is coming to Boston to do some background work, and knows this assignment is not going to be easy. Harry has been sent from Chicago to organize the cabdrivers of Boston into a local chapter of the Teamsters.

Harry is a gruff Vietnam Vet. His remaining thin, wavy grey hair is unkempt. He is fit, in his late fifties, and dressed in a dark, wrinkled three-piece suit. The tie has been removed, and is in his pocket.

Benjamin has sprung from his bed. Hung over, he hurriedly stumbles into in his chauffer's outfit that had been cast in a pile on the bedroom floor. He hops across the room on, and in, one leg, to the bathroom, quickly brushes his teeth and runs a hand across his hair.

Benjamin slips across to the bath, finds Amy, kisses her squarely on the forehead and says, "I love you".

Karen has her eyes closed, while she continues to bubble away. She smiles as she is kissed. Then she quickly sits up and frowns, "Hey, you, where do you think you're going?"

Benjamin, while headed out of the bathroom and toward the apartment door, responds.

"Sorry, Aim… I forgot to tell you… I promised to cover an important driving gig today. I'm late… I'll call you from the car."

"But you promised to spend the day with me!"

Benjamin does not respond. He hurries through the door, soars down the stairs, pulling on his coat on the fly, and shoulders his way out the front door. Quickly, he unlocks the frozen door of the black sedan parked on the street out front. He puts the key in the ignition, turns the key and…

He never hears the sound of the explosion, but only senses a soft, falling whiteness of hot snow. The limousine is transformed into thousand small, projected samples of metal, glass, rubber, leather, and Benjamin. There is nothing left but a heap of twisted metal, and a fireball of joined remains.

Amy, submerged in her sad consternation below the tide-line of her bubble-bath, is shocked by a sharp crack and boom, and waves of vibration coming through cast-iron into her being, a monster trying to reach in and violently drown her from afar.

When Amy's system restores some reality to her senses, she lunges up from the tub, her only sudden thought, "Ben!"

Amy springs herself from the tub, skids across the tiles, and runs to the living room, seeing fire dancing in the reflection of the windows and throwing spastic shadows against the walls. Only a fireball below marks where Benjamin's car was parked. Horrified, she screams, "Ben! Benny!"

She knows he is gone.

Amy unleashes a horrified, broken scream, answering her awful realization that her loved one's remains are burning in the street below.

Across the Charles River

In Cambridge, Harry Sharpstone deports from his helicopter and heads into the Yellow Cab Company office. He is impatiently awaiting the arrival of his ride.

Harry had been attending a union banquet meeting on Friday night in Springfield, so the helicopter was the best mode for making this important early morning breakfast meeting here in Boston.

Harry was a tough, impatient sergeant in Vietnam. As a labor organizer, these traits have been helpful. "I've been waiting fifteen minutes," Harry muttered. "Who's Melio?" Harry asks in a sharp voice.

"That would be me," Melio responds.

"Hi Melio, I am Harry Sharpstone. Has my ride arrived yet? I'm on a tight schedule."

"Oh, hello, Mr. Sharpstone. It's nice to finally meet you in person."

Melio Rocco is the cab dispatcher, part-time cab driver, and the local organizer who requested that the Teamsters pursue unionizing the cab drivers.

"Ben's not here yet. I am very sorry, Mr. Sharpstone. I'll dispatch one of these cabs for you for the day right away. It's important for you to stay on schedule."

Several minutes later, Melio reports, "Sorry Mr. Sharpstone, since it is Saint Patricks Day, all scheduled drivers are real busy, and those who are not scheduled don't wanna to give up this day off. So I'm going to take you myself. I am your driver for the day."

"Alright, Melio. Let's get going."

Melio gets Harry across town to the Bayside Club in South Boston. This is no ordinary breakfast meeting. This is the annual Saint Patrick's Day breakfast, heavily attended every year by a who's who of Boston's most powerful politicians.

Saint Patricks's Day is a big event in every major city, but in Boston it is particularly special. In Boston, Saint Patrick's is also a legal holiday, as March 17th also happens to be Evacuation Day, the day the British fled Boston in defeat of the Revolutionary War. So today, all public offices are closed, and all the pubs are open.

Saint Patrick's Day means so much to State Senate President Billy Bulger that he was determined to find a way to make it a public holiday. Senator Bulger is also a historian. So, he scoured Boston history for an event that occurred on March 17th, and the evacuation of the British troops from Boston was just the perfect event to justify a government holiday celebration. And what sane politician would vote against making Saint Patrick's a holiday worthy of a day off and a public celebration?

The day's opening event, breakfast and a roast held at the Bayside Club, is hosted by none other than South Boston's own pinnacle of the political scene, State Senate President Billy Bulger. As president of the Senate, Bulger controls what bills are allowed to the floor for a vote. Even the Governor pays deference in order for his legislation to be brought to the Senate floor.

Senator Bulger has a sharp mental recollection of all favors extended to various politicians, and when the time is right to collect on a "favor", one can be sure that the payback will play strongly into the Senator's favor. As a result, the State payroll reads like a list of Bulger family, friends, neighbors and supporters.

But today isn't a day for political hardball. Today is time for camaraderie and good cheer. Today is a day for laughter, self-deprivation, stand-up comedy and a good-natured political roast. For Harry Sharpstone, this event is very important business. Today Harry gets to meet some of the political players who will be involved in both sides of the issue of the cabbie unionization process that is yet to begin.

Harry will study personalities, political associations, traits and just what makes each politician tick. Does he have an Achilles' heal? Who are friends and who are foes? Who can he trade favors with? What kind of favors will work to gain their support for his effort to unionize the cabdrivers? Ah yes, this is a busy morning for Harry, and a valuable opportunity.

As Harry enters the Bayside Club, an aide to Senator Bulger meets him. "Mr. Sharpstone?" The aide inquires.

"Yes," Harry responds.

"I am Clarence McDuff. Let me take you to meet Senator Bulger." He takes Harry to the side of the Head table and Senator Bulger comes over to meet him. "Senator Bulger, this is Mr. Sharpstone from the Teamsters Union, Chicago."

"Nice to meet you, Mr. Sharpstone", says Senator Bulger. "I apologize for not having any time to meet with you today. As I mentioned, I am the Master of Ceremonies here this morning."

"That is quite all right, Senator Bulger", Harry replies. "I appreciate the opportunity to attend this renowned event and I am sure this will be a valuable experience. I'll call your office on Monday to schedule a meeting with you."

"Wonderful, we'll talk again soon."

"Clarence, kindly show Mr. Sharpstone to his table."

Senator Bulger proceeds to the microphone to begin the breakfast (grace for the meal). Clarence takes Harry to his table. Harry sits down next a highly decorated police officer. He reaches to shake Harry's hand. "Hello, I'm Police Chief Bratton."

"It's very nice to meet you Chief Bratton. I'm Harry Sharpstone from the Chicago office of the Teamsters."

Senator Bulger, in a loud and jovial manner exclaims, "It's so nice to see Senator Kerry here. You were good to get here on time. Last year you were stuck in front of the mirror."

"Ah yes, I could never miss that red mop-headed Governor of ours. It's nice to see you, Governor Weld. I didn't know Protestants got up this early on the weekend. I understand your nature, as a former Federal Prosecutor, is as sharp as ever."

"It was only last week when he made a citizens' arrest. He pinched a handicapped person for parking in a regular parking spot."

"Nice collar there, Governor Weld. You are truly tough on crime."

"It's nice that the blue-blooded WASP could join us for the Feast of Saint Patrick. Corned beef and cabbage is hardly the Filet Mignon and asparagus that Governor Weld is accustomed to."

"American history is a favorite read for me. I recall in reading that the Welds came to Massachusetts in 1620 'with only the shirts on their backs'—and 8,000 pounds of gold. And they didn't arrive aboard the Mayflower. They sent their servants on the Mayflower to get the summer cottage ready."

"By the way, Governor, I received the House's 'no-new-taxes' budget yesterday. Of course I'm not done reviewing it for Senate consideration. What do you mean by 'no new taxes'? I could slap a tax on a galloping horse."

Senator Bulger looks toward the Governor's wife, Susan Weld, and says, "Don't be nervous. It is your husband we are after."

"OK Governor, before you have me removed, I surrender the floor. Ladies and Gentlemen, Governor Weld."

"Thank you, Senate president Bulger," exclaims Governor Weld in an equally loud and jovial manner.

"The Senate president is the only man I know who never uses a steak knife, but cuts his food with his tongue."

"You are right about that 'no-new-taxes' budget, Senator Bulger, it's been a tough couple of weeks for some of the Democrats in the Legislature. They have a recurring nightmare that the money they are spending is their own."

"I knew I still had a lot of work to do when I called Senator Bulger's office yesterday to confirm this gathering. The senator has a phone answering system with the following announcement: 'If you owe me a favor, press one and leave your number. I'll be sure to get right back to you. If I owe you a favor, hang up and wait for me to get back to you. If you wish to make a contribution to my campaign for reelection, press two and leave your credit card number. If you think Bill Weld is really running Massachusetts, press 3, leave your name and then press 2 and leave your credit card number.' Thank you very much."

Senator Bulger jumps up and retrieves the microphone from Governor Weld. "Oh yea, that was great, Governor. Hmmmmmm! If that's the best you can do, then my power position is safe for a long time."

Noticeably missing is Mayor Flynn. He is drawn to TV cameras the way moths are drawn to light. Ray Flynn just loves the klieg lights. He actually posed with Salman Rushdie.

Suddenly, Chief Bratton nudges Harry Sharpstone as he is completing a cell phone call. He leans over and speaks to Harry's ear "We need to talk. Please meet me in the entranceway." They get up and made their way to the rear of the hall.

"That was a detective from my office. Apparently a limousine blew up in Charlestown about one and half hours ago. The driver is dead. His girlfriend told the detective that he was driving for a teamsters organizer today as he left. Was this driver supposed to be working for you today?"

"Oh my goodness… why, yes, I believe so. I thought he overslept so I arranged another ride. I don't understand. Why would someone do this?"

"At this point, I do not know. The investigation is ongoing. Somehow, you could have been the actual target in this car bombing."

"Why would I be a target? I've just arrived. Who would be targeting me?"

"I do not know, but I am going to want to talk to you later this week. Are you planning to be in town for a while?"

After a pause for thought, Harry responds, "Yes I will be staying at the Bostonian this week. You can reach me there, Chief Bratton."

"Very good Harry, could I get your cell phone number?"

"Of course, it's 312-744-3334."

"Thank you, Mr. Sharpstone. I will follow up with you soon. "

In the meantime, former Governor Frank Seargant has been leading the crowd of four hundred in a series of Irish songs. Chief Bratton leaves the building and heads back to his command. Harry Sharpstone makes his way back to his table, where he takes his seat and resumes evaluating the room full of pols, the event, the culture, the politics and now the suspicious ties.

Now full of corned beef, cabbage, Irish whiskey, laughter and smiles, the mass of celebrants, celebrators and celebrities makes its way to strategic locations for viewing the Saint Patrick Day's parade.

Harry hops in his cab and is whisked off to the corner of "L" Street and East Broadway in South Boston. This is the former home of Cox Electric Company. Mr. Cox passed away several years ago. He learned his electrical skills firsthand from Thomas Edison, himself. The family still gathers here with his brethren of electricians for this annual parade tradition.

The union brothers have graciously reserved Harry a choice standing room position for the parade.

It's an ideal March day for this event. The temperature is 50 degrees and it is partly cloudy. It's a great day for a parade.

Boston's finest lead the way. The flags of the police color guard are unfurled and wave briskly in the cool breeze. Stationed on the corner right next to Harry is Sergeant Clancy O'Malley, who snaps to attention and salutes as the Color Guard marches by.

Suddenly, an approaching parade viewer who has "over celebrated" staggers close by, grabs the light pole on the corner, swings around and falls to the ground at Sergeant Clancy's feet, where he proceeds to expel his stomach contents onto the Officer's shoes. Sergeant Clancy flags down a police cruiser and they briskly deposit the drunken parade-goer into the cruiser and he is whisked away. While still there, the officers leave the Sergeant a towel to clean off his shoes. Clancy then sticks each foot in a nearby melting snow bank for the final rinse, and throws the towel into a nearby trashcan. It is now officially a good Saint Patrick's by all measures.

Meanwhile, sirens scream as police cruisers roll by.

They are followed by the high pitch of a bagpipes, fife and drum band. These burley men march strongly in their green plaid kilts. Next is the Grand Marshall. This year, Mayor Flynn is Grand Marshall. Mayor Flynn is known for frequently running in the Boston Marathon.

So, naturally, he chooses to walk the parade route, waving and shaking hands with the gathered citizens, while his family rides along behind him in a beautiful 1976 Cadillac Eldorado convertible.

A tremendous variety of marching bands, floats, and antique cars comprise the next forty minutes of parade display. The rear of the parade is comprised of a brigade of Boston's majestic Police horses. As they proceed by, a large deposit of horse manure is left behind, signaling the "official" end of the parade.

The crowd quickly disburses into the many neighborhood pubs to continue reveling in the daylong celebration of Irish Heritage. In Boston, on Saint Patrick's Day, everyone can be Irish.

While Harry was watching the parade, a middle-aged fellow approached him and introduced himself. "Hi Harry, I was keeping an eye out for you. I am Bernie Martin, the local steward of the electrician's union."

Bernie is a tired-looking, blue-collar kind of guy who may have grabbed one live wire too many. "I understand that you are looking to organize the cab drivers for unionization." Bernie hands Harry his business card. "Here is my number, feel free to give me call if I can be of any help."

"Thanks Bernie," Harry replies, "It looks like I will need all of the help I can get on this one. It sure helps to know who your friends are."

"I am headed inside. We have a hospitality area there and you are welcome to join me", says Bernie.

"Thanks," says Harry, and they proceed inside.

As Harry and Bernie enter the hall, it dawns on that Harry that this town is all about who you know. Any contact and every contact may become a handy contact at any given time in this campaign.

This gathering is a who's who of various union officials that are all well-connected in Boston. Harry asks Bernie to introduce him to the gathering, one on one. As they proceed through the group in attendance, Harry is careful to exchange business cards and pleasantries with all of them. This has turned out to be a valuable day of "learning the landscape" for Harry.

Suddenly, it occurs to Harry, that his original driver, Barry Blumberg, had been blown to bits earlier today and if he were not running late, he would have been blown to bits too.

It's now about 3:30 P.M.

"Bernie," Harry exclaims, "you have been a big help to me today and I have had a great time. I have other business matters to check on. I have to get going. I will be in touch, brother."

"OK brother," Bernie responds. "We are always ready to help our union brethren. Bye for now."

Harry starts making his way out of the gathering and calls his driver, Melio on the cell phone. "Hey Melio, meet me out front in five minutes."

When Harry gets in the cab he says to Melio "let's head over to Barry Blumberg's place. I'll explain on the way over."

Melio is a little confused, but Melio sometimes has trouble reading a lottery scratch ticket, so his confusion is not unexpected.

Harry tells Melio about Barry's gangland-style death.

Melio is shocked, scared, upset, angered, and saddened by this story. He gradually grabs the steering wheel and depresses the gas pedal harder and harder as they head in express fashion from South Boston to Barry's place in Charlestown.

Ah yes, Charlestown.

It's across the Charles River from Boston's North End, South and West of the Mystic River and East of Cambridge and Route 93, an isolated neighborhood of Boston known as the site of the famous Battle of Bunker Hill, the home of the Bunker Hill Monument, the Boston Shipyard and the Navy's oldest active vessel, 'Old Ironsides'.

Charlestown is a hilly area with rows of brownstones leading down toward the Charles River. Charlestown is remote from Boston's downtown areas yet it is rich with Boston 's colonial history and modern day industrial businesses.

Charlestown is a blue-collar neighborhood settled mostly by Italian immigrants and maintains its strong Italian heritage today.

And yes, Charlestown is the home of the Boston Chapter of the Italian mob, much like South Boston is the home of Boston's Irish mob.

Boston is truly a cultural melting pot. As Boston's diverse populations all struggle for cultural dominance, its political neighborhood boundaries frequently serve as its cultural neighborhood boundaries. These boundaries, while generally respected, only stand as a frame for cultural identity.

Today, on Saint Patrick's day, Boston's homogeneous population celebrates together as one great city, with culture to boot.

When approaching Barry's address, Harry tells Melio, "Drive down the street slowly so I can check this out. Then head around the block and park two or three doors before Barry's address."

Melio parks on the right side of the street diagonally across from Barry's former home. There is a police car parked three cars head of them.

Apparently, they are keeping an eye on this crime scene for further developments. Harry just might be one of those developments.

"OK Melio, I'm going to go check on the scene. Then I'm going in to meet Barry's girlfriend and see what else I can find out. Give me a call if something comes up."

"Like what?"

"I don't know, but I guess you'll know it when you see it."

Harry strolls over to the area out front of Barry's address. It's been about nine hours since the explosion. So, naturally the damaged car (s) and other debris has been cleaned up and removed.

All that remains is a chalk outline of where Barry's remains were found, which is within an area marked off with yellow police caution tape. Harry breathes a sigh of shock and relief. There is only one chalk outline. It looks like only one person was killed in the blast.

Harry shakes his lowered head in sadness and confusion. Why? What was meant by this? Did Barry have a checkered past? Did he have enemies? Was this meant for me, or was this meant to be a message to me? There are lots of questions that need answers.

Harry looks up at the police cruiser across the street. They are observing Harry, and paying careful attention to him, but they are not approaching him.

Harry turns and heads into the building. He stops at the top of the stairs and rings the doorbell. Karen Silkstocking answers the bell. She responds in a sobbing voice.

"Who is it?"

"My name is Harry Sharpstone. Barry was on his way to meet me this morning. May I come in?"

There is a long pause. Then the door buzzer goes off. Harry goes in and proceeds up the stairs to the third floor. The door at the top of the landing is open slightly. Harry slowly and respectfully goes in and closes the door. He can see a woman sitting in a wing chair in the living room in her bathrobe, sobbing.

"Hello, I'm Harry Sharpstone."

Without looking up or toward Harry, Karen responds. "Hello Harry, I'm Karen Silkstocking. Come on in and have a seat."

Karen is obviously in shock. Harry proceeds in slowly and quietly sits down.

"Ms. Silkstocking, I'm very sorry for your loss. While I did not know Barry, I planned to work with him in the coming weeks. I have no idea why this happened or who would do such a thing. I was hoping to get some answers from you."

"I don't know anything," Karen sharply responded. "We planned to spend the day together until he got the unexpected assignment to drive for you. Who are you anyway and what are you doing here. Are you some sort of big shot? Are you a crook? A mobster? Why did I even let you in? Am I in danger? Oh my goodness, I'm in danger right? Are you here to kill me?"

"Please calm down Ms. Silkstocking. I am not going to hurt you. I am also confused. I am just looking for answers. Maybe you can help me process this and I can help you process this as well."

There is a pause. Karen says, "I'm sorry, but I am so confused. Can I get you a cup of coffee?"

"That would be great."

"Is instant OK?"

"That will be fine."

Karen saunters off to the kitchen and starts making instant coffee.

"Ms. Silkstocking."

"Please call me Karen."

"OK, Karen", Harry continues, "Please can you tell me what happened this morning? Take your time."

"It was just before 7:00 A.M. I was up early taking a bath. Barry was still asleep. He had worked late last night. He had promised to spend the day with me. I was so excited. Just me and Barry, spending all of Saint Patrick's Day together. We were going to go to the parade and just celebrate all day long.

"Suddenly, the phone rang. Barry sprang up, got dressed and dashed out the door. He was saying that he had to go and he would make it up to me. Now I was furious. I jumped out of the tub, grabbed a towel, and ran to the window. I threw open the window and

"… then there was a loud boom, a gust of wind, a big fire flash and metal debris and smoke everywhere. I was shocked and horrified. As the smoke cleared I saw Barry's car in a tangled mess of scrap down below. I knew that Barry had to be inside. I started screaming. I was screaming, screaming like I had never screamed before.

"Then, I called 911. I reported the car explosion. I was shocked and paralyzed. I was too paralyzed and shocked to move. I was scared. I was too scared to go downstairs and see what I might see. I knew it. I just knew it. I knew that Barry was dead. I just knew that my man was dead. I could not go down because I could not bare to see what I might see."

Harry stands up. Karen grabs Harry by the shoulders. "Do you know what I mean Harry? I could not handle this. The police, fire and EMT's were here very fast. They were here right away. I just rolled up in a ball in this chair. I could not look. I just could not look."

Karen is now sobbing. There is a pause. Then Karen brings the instant coffee out to the living room and serves Harry and herself.

"Thank you, Karen. Thank you for the coffee and thank you for telling me the details of your day. You have truly had a day of horror and shock beyond anything that I can imagine. Please sit down and try to calm down a little. Apparently, Barry's demise was meant for me as well. But I do not know why."

"Well, why are you here Mr. Sharpstone?"

"Karen, you can call me Harry. I am here from Chicago. I am a union organizer. I was assigned to organize the Boston area Cab drivers into a union."

The two of them are drinking their coffee.

Then Karen exclaims, "Oh My gosh. Barry told me that the cab drivers were upset about how poorly they are treated and how little say they have in their business. He mentioned that they were going to organize into a union. He also mentioned that there would be resistance to a union. He said it could be a very nasty fight to unionize."

"Well, there is almost always is a bitter fight in the unionization process" says Harry. "But this is a real early and strong message."

"Barry said that in Boston the Chief of Police is in charge of controlling the taxi medallions," continues Karen. "He said that is because their issuance is considered a safety matter here."

"What?" exclaims Harry. "I have never heard of a city where the Chief of Police controls the taxi medallions. That is interesting. Karen, thank you very much. Please get some rest. You have been a big help. Do you have a friend to come stay with you?"

"Yes, my friend will be here soon."

"Great. I am very sorry for your loss. Are arrangements being made for Barry?"

"We plan to work all of that out tomorrow."

"OK, Karen, here is my card. Please call me if I can be of any help. May I have your number?"

"Yes, it is 617-327-7306."

The two of them politely shake hands and Harry leaves.

It is now 6:00 P.M. It has been a long day. When Harry reaches the car, Melio, the lookout driver, has fallen asleep. Harry wakes Melio up, hops in the car and says, "why don't you drop me off at the Bostonian Hotel and we will call it a day."

When Harry and Melio arrive at the Bostonian Hotel, there is an unmarked police car parked near the main entrance. The two plainclothes officers inside try not to look toward Harry as he heads into the hotel; however, Harry is now keenly aware that he is under surveillance.

"Melio, our organizational meeting is scheduled for tomorrow at Four P.M at the yellow cab garage. How many drivers will be attending?"

"I expect about one hundred drivers."

"That's a great start."

"I'll have a cab here to pick you up at three-thirty."

"That will be great. Now go get some rest. Our meeting tomorrow will probably have some high energy. Good night, Melio."

"Good Night."

Harry quickly goes into the hotel and after dinner he retires in his room for the day.

Melio heads home to get some rest.

It's Sunday

Since it is the day after Saint Patrick's Day, Boston has a hangover. Harry spends the morning preparing his thoughts and remarks for the four o'clock meeting. At noon Harry decides to head across the street to the Faniuel Hall marketplace and grab some lunch and a dose of Boston Culture.

Faniuel Hall is a walking retail marketplace and a favorite stop for tourists in Boston. There are many vendors selling everything from North End pizza to New York Deli, to Asian cuisine, to New England clam chowder. There are also numerous merchants selling everything from coffee mugs, tee shirts and sweatshirts to fine artwork and jewelry. This is ground zero for purchasing a memento of your trip to Boston.

Meanwhile street entertainers ranging from jugglers and storytellers to string quartets and brass ensembles perform cheerfully for the masses of smiling tourists. This is truly one of Boston's gems where happiness, culture, and commerce abounds.

Harry gradually melts into the scene. The afternoon drifts by in the spectacle of this daily outdoor festival. As Harry realizes that it is about three o'clock, he makes his way back to the Bostonian Hotel to await the arrival of his ride to Cambridge.

Melio pulls up in front of the Bostonian. As Harry steps into the cab, he notices a different unmarked police cruiser out front. Police surveillance continues. Harry and Melio head off to the meeting at Yellow Cab Company in Cambridge.

"Harry, the word of Barry Blumberg being blown to bits has spread throughout the group of cab drivers. Thoughts, and tensions are running high. I just thought you should have an idea of what to expect."

"Thanks Melio. Are arrangements for Barry complete?"

"Yes… (Melio pauses in a sullen manner)… the wake is going to be tomorrow from four to seven at the Carr Funeral Home in Charlestown. The Funeral is scheduled for Ten o'clock on Tuesday Morning. You can ride with me."

"Thank you Melio. By the way, please let the family know that the Union has agreed to pick up the cost of Barry's funeral."

"Harry, that is very generous. They have no money. I'll be sure to let them know."

Suddenly, Harry's cell phone rings. "Hello, Mr. Sharpstone, it's Chief Bratton."

"Why hello Chief Bratton. What's up?"

"I am trying to put the pieces together on the car bombing which killed Barry Blumberg. Are you free to have coffee with me at nine o'clock tomorrow morning so we can discuss this incident? "

"Chief Bratton, I'll plan to be in your office tomorrow at nine o'clock sharp. Thank you for calling. Good afternoon."

Melio exclaims, "I'll meet you at 8:30 A.M. in front of the Bostonian."

"Thanks Melio."

"No, don't thank me. I need to do this. Barry was a good friend. I made the call to you that put this whole process in motion. This issue is just too important. I'm on board with you all the way, Harry."

Just then, they pull up in front of the Yellow Cab garage. As Harry is getting out of the cab he exclaims to Melio, "The challenge is on. Let's get this organization going."

As they enter the garage the mood of the large crowd gathered is evident. Melio walks to a position near the office from where he can address the gathering. The group gathered is nearly all men. All nationalities and all age groups are represented. About fifty drivers are seated. The rest are standing. We have a full house.

"Hey guys, pipe down," Melio starts in. "By now you've all heard about Barry Blumberg. Barry's wake is tomorrow from four to seven at the Carr Funeral home. The Funeral is on Tuesday at Ten o'clock. It goes without sayin' but lets get as many of the cabbies to turn out and pay him some respect as possible. So spread the word. I'm not good at this group talking stuff so I'm gonna turn the meeting over to Harry Sharpstone. He's a Union organizer from the teamsters in Chicago."

"Thanks Melio," starts Harry. "Melio contacted us and told me of your situation. The way I understand it is Cab Medallions are controlled by a very few fat cat investors. So there is no opportunity... (pause) there is no opportunity for you folks to negotiate for better earnings or move forward and own your own cab. Beyond that you must pay rent for your cab shift with no certainty of fares to cover your rent... no certainty of fares to pay for your apartment rent... no certainty of money for groceries or healthcare. This is what I am here to change." Big applause from the gathering.

"Tell us more Harry," responds someone from the crowd. "Yea, yea tell us more" yell a few more.

"All right," Harry starts in. "I am here to help you with these circumstances. I am here to tell you that you can achieve a better deal and I am here to help you achieve that better deal. There is strength in numbers and I feel the strength of this group here tonight. Individually, we have no ability to affect change, but as a group united...

"... as an organized group of many our strength is evident and it will prevail. I am here to organize this group. I am here to form this group into a union chapter and as a chapter of the teamsters our national strength will be evident. Our strength will have to be reckoned with. With our national strength we will be able to negotiate and achieve a better financial position and a better quality of life for all of you. Are you with me? Will you stand with Melio and me and the strength that the teamsters union brings to the table?"

A loud crescendo of sustained positive enthusiasm, and spontaneously, a loud prolonged chant of "Teamsters Union" fills the garage.

Harry feels the energy and senses that this group is ready and he can get this unionization done.

"Okay guys, lets continue," yells Harry. "Now this is not going to be easy but I sense this group is ready to get this done."

"Yea, yea," responds the crowd.

"Okay," Harry barks. "Okay," (in a softer voice) "I am excited about this too but we must calm down a little so I can continue here. First I need to get some basic information from all of you. I have six pads of paper up here on this table. As you leave tonight stop by the table and write down your name, address and telephone number."

"I sense we are up against a strong resistance. This resistance has already made a move. Barry Blumberg was supposed to pick me up on Saturday when his car blew up. Folks, this was no accident. Thank goodness Barry was running a little late or I would have been blown up with him. This does not scare me. I do not back down. We will prevail. I don't know who was behind this bomb blast but I plan on working with Chief Bratton to get to the bottom of this."

"If any of you has information that you think may be helpful in solving this tragedy, please see me after the meeting or simply take my business card off the table and give me a call at your earliest convenience. I am sure we will get to the bottom of this. I am sure we will find Barry's killer. Tomorrow evening let's turn out in a big way and pay our last respects to Barry. Then, on Tuesday, I hope that as many of you that can make it to his funeral show up. Tuesday at four o'clock, let's all meet back here again and we will begin to plan our move forward…

"I chose four o'clock so that we are on a shift change, and more drivers can attend that way. In the meantime, contact as many cabbies as possible and spread the word about the four o'clock meeting. At that time, we will select an organizer-leader from each cab company. If you can select your garage leader before the meeting, that would be great. The meeting will move along that much quicker and smoother."

"Thanks for all for coming out. I'll see all of you at the wake, the funeral, and then at the next meeting. Now come up to the table and sign in before you leave."

A positive energy fills the garage as the group moves forward to sign in and then slowly starts to disperse.

The crowd completes its sign in and disperses. Melio looks at Harry with a grin on his face.

"Unbelievable. Harry, you were great. This is gonna happen. It's really gonna happen."

"Melio, I can't do this without you. I need you at my side. You are my connection to the group. You have all of the local knowledge. You have a big role to play in this. Are you ready for it?"

"I'm ready, man. I am ready. I am all in."

Meanwhile, Harry has picked up all of the sign in sheets.

"Good," he says, "Now let's get of here."

Harry and Melio leave the garage. As they head towards Melio's cab Harry notices yet another unmarked cruiser parked across the street from the garage. He senses that this is more than just standard procedure surveillance. This is more like prime suspect surveillance, but prime suspect of what? He just can't quite put his finger on what is going on. Does Chief Bratton's control over medallions have something to do with this? Who could have placed that bomb in Barry's car? These questions are running through Harry's mind. Harry and Melio reach Melio's cab, hop in and drive back to the Bostonian Hotel.

As they head back into Boston, Melio breaks the silence. "Hey Harry, have you noticed that a police cruiser shows up almost everywhere we go? What's up with that?"

"I don't know, Melio, so you noticed all of the police protection too."

"Oh yea, and it's got me thinkin', why are we getting all of this police attention?"

"Well, Melio, as you know Chief Bratton controls of the medallions. The word must be out that I am in town to organize the cabbies. All I can figure is the medallion owners have their police force keeping an eye on me. By this time I'm sure they are also keeping an eye on you too my friend. My thought is that Chief Bratton has a closer relationship to the medallion owners than he probably should. I hope I am wrong about that. Gaud, I hope I am wrong."

"In the meantime, get some rest, Melio, and I will see you tomorrow morning for a ride to Chief Bratton's Office. Be careful. Good night."

Harry hops out of the cab and heads directly into the hotel. He realizes that his meeting with Chief Bratton could be quite intense.

IV

Monday morning

Harry arrives at Chief Bratton's office at nine o'clock sharp. Harry is shown directly into Chief Bratton's office.

"Good morning, Mr. Sharpstone, come on in and have a seat."

"Thank you, Chief Bratton, please call me Harry."

"I'm pouring coffee, Harry, how do you take it?"

"Black."

"I'm very sorry about the death of Barry Blumberg. I did not know him. However, I understand he was on his way to pick you up for your day of activities."

"That's right. Can you tell me any more?"

"Such as… ?"

"Such as, do you know of anyone who would want to kill you or Barry? Why would someone want to kill you or Barry? What is going on to trigger such violence?"

"Actually, Chief Bratton, I was hoping that you could answer those questions for me. As you know, I'm in town to assist the cab drivers in resolving the frustrations they bear as a result of being a disorganized a work force."

"Well," isn't that just a clever way of suggesting that you are here to organize the cab drivers into a labor union?"

"I am still examining their plight; however, organizing the group into a union may be an option to cure their frustrations."

"Hmmm, I see, and are any other solutions being considered?"

"Chief Bratton, I thought this meeting was about solving the murder of Barry Blumberg. You seem to be moving into another area altogether."

"Well, Harry, one never knows just what information may be a clue, now does one?"

"Chief Bratton, would you be referring to the information that you are solely responsible for the awarding of medallions in Boston?"

"Where are you going with that?"

"Well I'm sure that anything that may weaken the dominance of the medallion owners will also affect the value of the medallions, their resulting business and maybe the entire management perspective of the cab industry."

"Harry, I simply control the medallions for the safety perspective."

"I see… and is the constant surveillance purely for my safety as well?"

"Absolutely, Harry, you were possibly a target of that car bomb. I have no leads. Someone may still be out for you. I would be very careful if I were you. And I will continue to protect you to the best of my ability. But even the best of abilities is not always enough. So I would be very careful."

"I see… thank you for your advice. Is there anything else Chief Bratton?"

"Going forward I will not be able to comment on our ongoing investigation. Please, take my card. If you come across any information that could help us solve this case, please call me directly, right away. I assure you Harry, the actions of this police department are always focused toward maintaining the law, order, and public safety."

"That's great, Chief. I appreciate all that you and the police department are doing to solve this terrible murder and provide me with safety surveillance. Thank you for the coffee. I'll be on my way. Good day."

"Thank you for stopping by, Harry."

As Harry leaves Chief Bratton's office, there are about a half dozen news reporters looking for information about the car bombing on Saturday.

"Hey", shouts out a reporter, "I think he's the guy. He's the guy that was waiting for that car to pick him up!"

The reporters quickly surround Harry and start chattering rapid-fire questions at him.

Harry states, "I am not answering any questions today. Today and tomorrow are about paying final respects to a dedicated cab driver and a fine person, Barry Blumberg. I call on you to respect my privacy during these days of sadness and reflection. In exchange, I will grant you an opportunity to ask questions on Friday morning at eleven o'clock. I will be in the entrance circle area out front of the Bostonian Hotel and I will have a statement for you at that time. Thank you."

As the chatter of questions pipes up again, Harry makes a quick exit, down the stairs, out the front door and into Melio's waiting cab.

"Let's move" Harry says to Melio.

"What's up Harry?"

"I sense our activity is drawing strong interest, both pro and con."

"No kidding."

"What do you mean, Melio?"

"Well Harry, while you were in that meeting, I was listening to the cabbie radio talk."

"And… ?"

"And, I think we are going to need a bigger garage for the meeting tomorrow."

"Noooo Kidding. OK, let me take care of that."

Harry pulls out his cell phone and the business card of Bernie Martin, the Electrical Union steward. "Hello, Bernie. Harry Sharpstone calling."

"Yea Mr. Sharpstone, what's up?"

"Well, Bernie, I'm glad you asked. I've got a meeting planned for four o'clock on Tuesday afternoon. Bernie, the group is going to be larger than I expected. Can you help me out?"

"Sure Mr. Sharpstone. No problem. You can use the electrician's union hall in Dorchester. I'll have it all set up to seat about three hundred and coffee for the guys."

"That's great, Bernie I have one more favor to ask."

"Fire away, Harry."

"Bernie, I'm sure that the local electrical workers have an attorney who is well versed in state and federal union law."

"Yes we do, Harry. As a matter of fact he is my brother, Tim Martin. Would you like his number?"

"Yes I would, Bernie."

"OK, it's 617-742-0615. Tell him I said 'hi'."

"Bernie, thanks for coming through."

"Hey, glad to help. That's what it's all about."

"See you tomorrow, Bernie."

"Ten-four good buddy. Over and out."

Bernie is a former CB Radio aficionado and an avid ham radio buff.

Harry calls Attorney Tim Martin. "Hello, is this Attorney Martin?"

"Yes it is. And who is this?"

"My name is Harry Sharpstone. Your brother Bernie gave me your number."

"I see. How can I help?"

"Thanks Mr. Martin. I am an organizer for the Teamsters Union. I am here to organize the taxi cab drivers. I will certainly need local legal guidance and representation. I suspect that as the counsel for the electrical workers, you are one of the best qualified in this field in greater Boston."

"Why thank you Mr. Sharpstone. Union representation is one of my areas of specialty."

"Excellent. I am having an organizational meeting on Tuesday at 4:00 P.M at the electrician's union hall. I hope you can join us at that time. Naturally, you will be paid for your time."

"Mr. Sharpstone, I'll plan on being there. I look forward to taking on this important effort."

"That's great, Mr. Martin. I look forward to meeting you. And please call me Harry."

"Thanks Harry. Please call me Tim. I'll see you Tuesday."

"OK, Melio. Do you know where the electrician's union hall is in Dorchester?"

"Hey, I'm a cabbie. Of course I know where it is."

"Good. Then get on the radio and let the guys know that the meeting has been moved. It is going to be at the electrician's union hall Tuesday at four, and their attendance is important."

"Gotcha, Harry. And I'll pick you up about four o'clock for Barry's wake. Now I've gotta go make some fares."

"Thanks, Melio. See you at four."

Harry jumps out of the cab, and once again notices the police presence. He wonders, are they really there for his protection, or are they surveilling him for something else? He hopes he can trust Chief Bratton, but Harry's no fool. After all, he's a labor organizer from Chicago. He's knows that there is no honor amongst thieves, criminals, crooks and thugs.

One minute criminals are out working on a "job" together and are as close as twin brothers. The next time out one "brother" is plugging two bullets in the back of the head of the other. Harry just shakes his head and thinks "Man… Boston is just as much of a jungle as Chicago."

Harry heads to his room. On the way, he decides to give State Senator Billy Bulger's office a call.

Harry enters his room and pulls out his cell phone.

"Senator Bulger's office… "

"Ah, hello sir, this is Harry Sharpstone calling. Senator Bulger is expecting my call."

"Very good Mr. Sharpstone, one minute please… "

"Hello, Mr. Sharpstone, Bill Bulger here. How can I help?"

"Thanks for taking my call, Senator. I wanted to let you know that I am having a union organization meeting at the electrician's Union hall on Tuesday at 4:00 P.M."

"I see."

"That's right, and I understand that you are considered to be a strong advocate of union positions."

"I see."

"I wanted you to know that in light of your support it would be great if you could appear at the meeting."

"I see. This sounds quite interesting. I cannot commit. However, I'll certainly keep it in mind."

"I see. Thank you, Senator. By the way, you mentioned that we should get together this week for a meeting."

"Why yes, Mr. Sharpstone, of course. Shall we say Wednesday morning at 9:30 A.M. in my Senate office?"

"Nine thirty sharp on Wednesday, it is."

"Thank you for calling, Mr. Sharpstone."

"Thank you for taking my call, Senator Bulger."

It is interesting that the simple two-word phrase "I see" can have so many meanings.

Four O'clock Sharp

Melio roles up in front of the Bostonian Hotel. Harry jumps in the back seat. The radio is on.

"Thank you caller… and now it's time for Listo Fisher with the news. I'm Howie Carr."

Howie Carr is the afternoon drive-time talk-show host on WRKO in Boston. Howie has also been a political reporter for the Boston Herald for many years. He also is the go-to reporter for organized crime activity in Boston.

Howie has had his life threatened by known crime boss and FBI most-wanted Whitey Bulger of South Boston. Oh yea, Whitey's brother just happens to be President of the State Senate, Billy Bulger. That's right. The President of the State Senate and the FBI most-wanted crime boss are brothers. A fiction writer could not make this one up. It's incredibly convenient that one reporter covers both the political scene and the crime scene. Somehow, they seamlessly cross paths.

The radio news continues

"Saturday there was a car explosion on High Street in Charlestown. The driver, Barry Blumberg, a long time Boston cab driver, was the only fatality. He will be put to rest on Tuesday. There was no one else in the car. Police are tight-lipped on what their investigation has revealed other than to say that the incident is being treated as a homicide. And that's the news at four. And now back to 'The Howie Carr Show'… …

"Thanks Listo," Howie starts. "That last story has certainly peaked my interest. That is quite a news story. I'm sure we will be hearing more about that. As we say in the Biz, that story 'has legs'. This is 'The Howie Carr Show'."

"Let's make that last news story the topic of discussion for the top of this hour's callers. What do you think is the story behind the story? Why was this cabbie a target? Was this a mob hit? Why? Now back to the phones."

"Angelo from Charlestown, you're first up this hour. What do you think? Was that car bomb a mob hit?"

"Ahhh yea right, I think it was hit."

"Why do you say that Angelo?"

"Because I know."

"What do you know Angelo?"

"Look, I know these cabbies have been talking some smack lately and this is the way the boys send 'em a message to stay in line."

"What do you mean Angelo? What kinda smack has been going down and just who are these 'boys' that you mention?"

"Well, ya know, the cabbies have been talking about unionizing or someth'n and the cab owners and medallion owners are probably kinda upset about that or someth'n."

"Shut that off, Melio. I've heard enough. What can we expect at the wake"

"Well Harry, from the radio chatter it sounds like there will be a big cabbie turnout. I've arranged back door parking and access for us. Karen Silkstocking has asked if you would stand with her and the family."

As they approach the Funeral home, there are taxi cabs parked everywhere. There is a waiting line out the front door and down the sidewalk to pay their final respects to their fallen friend. Melio parks next to the back door, and the two slip in the back entrance. Harry takes a position next to Karen Silkstocking and the closed casket and begins acknowledging the mourners.

"Oh Harry, thank you for being here with me. I could not stand here by myself, and I really don't know Barry's family that well."

Barry did not have any children. His father passed away in a construction fall at the shipyard ten years ago. It was deemed to be an accident.

Now that Barry has died in such a murderous way, Barry's family wonders if his father's death was an accident or just made to look like an accident. The details of his father's death were always unclear. The shipyard's insurance company stepped forward quickly to establish an annuity which seemed to be comfortable money for Mrs. Blumberg at that time. However, by today's standards it amounts to a pile of crumbs.

Why has their family been marked with these two tragedies? Such questions are often asked times like these and are almost never answered.

Barry also has a younger sister, Amelia. She was married four years ago to Charlie Hartbody. Charlie is a Gulf War Marine veteran and he works full time for the Veterans Administration as a physical therapist and disabled veteran caseworker. Amelia is a teaching assistant in the local school system but is presently on maternity leave as the couple had their first child, Charlie junior, just two months ago. They have had the happiest four years as a married couple as any couple could want. The arrival of baby Charlie has been a big shining moment for them and grandma Blumberg.

Suddenly, Amelia has become severely grief stricken by the loss of her brother. Charlie is sad and angry. He is angry that Barry died in such a manner. At this sensitive time Charlie's thoughts of somehow avenging his brother-in-law's death emphasize just how sad, angry and yet frustrated he truly is. They were not close, but the grief realized by his wife and mother-in-law leaves him feeling that he somehow must try to help relieve them of this grief. While he does his best to comfort them and assist them, he is frustrated because somehow he feels he should be doing more.

Karen Silkstocking introduces Harry to Barry's family. Harry expresses his condolences to the family. As they realize who he is, they react quite coldly to Harry's presence at Barry's wake.

Mrs. Blumberg exclaims, "Thank you for your expression of sympathy. But where do I get my son back? Why did you put his life in jeopardy? Why did you have to bring your Chicago mobster ways here to Charlestown? Why has my family been the target of these violent deaths?"

"I'm very sorry for your loss, Mrs. Blumberg… " Harry realizes that there is nothing more he can say so he solemnly moves away.

Karen Silkstocking follows Harry to the side.

"It's obvious that standing there is not the right thing for me to do, Karen. I'll just stay nearby, we can talk later. You should stay there with the Blumberg family."

"I understand. "But please don't leave. I need to talk to you."

"I'll wait here."

"Thank you," she responds, and then returns to be with Barry's family.

Harry scopes out the room. It is abundant with a large variety of flower arrangements and spiritual bouquets. The line of mourners continues to move along, and the room fills with small groups of conversationalists reflecting on their relationship to their fallen friend. The group gathered is dominated by cab drivers. Cab driving was Barry's life, and the cab drivers had become his closest family.

City counselor "Dapper O'Neill" passes through the line and past the coffin. He is truly a man of the people. Even at his advanced age, he has been known to chase down a purse-snatcher, tackle him, and hold him at gunpoint until the police arrived. He is known for being a loud voice and strong advocate on behalf of the people in the City Council chambers.

Mayor Flynn also files by the coffin and pays his respects.

It has been a long evening. Karen Silkstocking approaches Harry.

"Harry," Karen says slowly, "I'm not dealing well with this. I just cannot stay in Barry's bed tonight. I have nowhere to go. Can you help me?"

Harry puts his hand on her shoulder and says, "I understand. Do you have a friend you can stay with?"

"My friends are willing but they all live in small places and really don't have any room for me."

"Karen, I'll provide you a room at the Bostonian tonight. Melio and I will take you by your place and you can pack a bag for tonight and the funeral tomorrow."

"Thank you, Harry. Thank you."

Harry, Melio and Karen head outside and notice flashing emergency lights all over the area. But they aren't blue police lights. They are yellow tow-truck lights. They get into Melio's car and head over to a tow-truck. Melio stops and asks a tow-truck driver "Hey driver, what's going on?"

The driver responds, "It looks like about thirty or forty cabs had their tires slashed during the wake."

All around, cabs are being towed away and drivers are hitching rides home from the more fortunate drivers. The reactions are high-tempered. Harry realizes that tomorrow's meeting attendance and tension has just been ratcheted up.

Who's behind this slashed tire incident? Is it the cab owners and medallion holders? Sure they would like to let the drivers know that they are firmly in control, but would they damage their own cars to send them this message? Is it Chief Bratton conveying the message for the owners? Why would he incite a public crime? Have the owners gotten to Billy Bulger? Could Harry himself have arranged the tire slashing in order to get the cab drivers charged up for tomorrow's meeting? Someone is sending a message, but what is the message, and who is sending it?

Melio's cab pulls up to Karen's brownstone. She heads in and quickly packs for over night. They drive off to the Bostonian, and check Karen in.

Melio heads home.

Harry and Karen head across the street to Fanueil Hall for a quiet dinner. Then it is back to the hotel and the two retire for the day.

Tomorrow is certain to be another day of high emotion.

8:30 Tuesday morning

Harry and Karen are out front and ready as Melio pulls up in front of the Bostonian. They get into the cab and off they go to the Funeral Parlor. It is a mild sunny March day. The Funeral proceedings are incident free. Harry is laid to rest.

Karen's emotions run high, understandably. There are about one hundred people in attendance. About ninety of those are cab drivers. The rest are close family members. Most of the group moves to the Yellow Cab garage after the burial for a luncheon buffet provided by the cab company.

Harry decides not to attend. He is concerned that by now the Yellow Cab Company ownership is on to his intentions. Melio gives him a ride back to the Bostonian.

Karen feels well enough to return to her apartment and begin to sort out her future.

Harry decides to take in a workout and prepare his thoughts for the four o'clock meeting.

At about three P.M Melio arrives at the Bostonian. Harry is ready to go. He is dressed in a dark blue pinstripe suit with a white shirt and a red striped tie. The tie is tied loosely and the top button is unbuttoned. Nevertheless, Harry is confident that he was ready.

He gets into the cab just as the news is playing on the radio. "… cab drivers are upset by the vandalism that occurred last night. About thirty cabs had their tires slashed while their drivers were attending the wake of a slain cab driver in Charlestown last evening. If you have any information that leads to the capture of these vandals…

"… Yellow Cab is offering a thousand dollar reward for information leading to their arrest and conviction. Now back to 'The Howie Carr Show…'"

"Thanks Listo. This is 'The Howie Carr Show' and I am Howie Carr." Howie takes an unusually long pause. "Folks, something large is in the wind here. We've had the violent death of a cab driver followed by this enormous act of vandalism on cabs while they were attending the fallen driver's wake. This is harsh. I hope that whatever this grudge is all about gets solved quickly in some meeting room. I trust that Chief Bratton has taken note, and that Boston's finest are on alert. Now…"

Melio turns off the radio. Shortly, they arrive at the Electricians Union Hall. The parking lot is full. Melio and Harry park.

Attorney Tim Martin is waiting outside the front door.

"Hello Harry, I'm Tim Martin."

Tim looks like a TV lawyer. He has a fit medium build, neat brown hair, and he is wearing a business suit.

Harry remarks, "Your Bernie's brother?"

Tim smiles and says, "Yes I am his brother, but we are not identical twins."

They share a laugh. Then Tim assumes his business demeanor. "It sounds like this will be an enthusiastic meeting. I suggest that I stand up front in case you want my legal input. We can take care of formalities another time, in a quieter environment."

"That sounds great. Tim, this is Melio. He made the initial contact with my office and has been a valuable wing man since my arrival."

The men exchange greetings. "He got us into this mess," Harry jokes. They all chuckle.

"Now let's go run a meeting."

The three men enter the union hall. The room is full to capacity. The crowd chatter is intense. It is obvious that this gathering is passionate, determined, and focused on a common goal, to form a union. Melio and Harry head directly to the front of the room. Harry motions Melio to introduce him. Melio goes up and takes the microphone.

"OK guys, let's quiet down so we can get this meeting started." The room noise quiets down quickly. "Harry Sharpstone, from Chicago, is here to run the meeting," continues Melio. "He is an organizer for the Teamsters Union." The room erupts in a roar of applause and shouts of support.

Harry steps up to the microphone.

"All right guys, I'm Harry Sharpstone. Save all that enthusiasm. We will need it." The room quiets down once again.

"Now, the purpose here tonight is to start the process of organization as a union. I have our attorney guiding the legal process. To my left is Attorney Tim Martin. He is attorney for the local electrician's union and has agreed to guide us through the legal components of this organizing procedure. I am informed by Attorney Martin that the course of process requires us to hold this informational meeting tonight. This meeting starts the thirty-day period between this initial meeting and the date to vote whether or not to unionize."

"I've asked that each garage select a steward. This steward will only stay in place until the election results are final, in thirty days. After that election, you will also vote for a steward for your garage. Anyone who wishes to run for steward, please take my business card tonight, and call my office in Chicago within the next week.

"They will take down the necessary information from you and your name will be placed on the ballot for your garage when we reach that point. Guys, this is not a time to be shy. This is the time to step up and be a leader. If you believe that you have what it takes then step forward. Your fellow drivers need you."

"If the vote is to unionize... "

The room erupts in a roar of cheering.

"OK... " Harry yells, "let's keep this meeting moving forward here."

The room quiets down.

"Thank you. If the vote is to unionize, I will meet with the newly elected stewards and they will elect a chapter president. I understand that there are five cab companies involved in this process. That's great.

At this time I would like to ask the five interim stewards please come up here to the front of the room."

Scattered applause and cheers of support fill the room. Melio, and four other drivers make their way to the head table. Harry gives each of them a member registration pad and a stack of his business cards and several pens. Then, he addresses the group again.

"OK, please note who the steward is for your cab company. Each one of them is going to a different area of the room. Please gather with them, fill out a place on the registration list, and take one of my business cards. You are all welcome to call me with any questions or concerns that may arise. This sign-in is important. Only those correctly signed-in here will be able to vote in thirty days. So fill it out carefully and correctly now."

The group follows Harry's instructions in an awkward but reasonably orderly manner.

"Listen up, while you are completing the registration. Since today is March 20th, the voting will take place here on Thursday April 19th from 8:00 A.M. to 8:00 P.M. There will be approved voting officials here to run the voting. The results will be announced at 9:00 P.M. the very same evening."

There is scattered applause once again, and Harry takes a brief pause, his mode suddenly changes, then he starts in again.

"In the meantime, I know we are all upset about Barry Blumberg's violent death and the tire slashings that took place during Barry's wake. You guys made a great showing of support at Barry's wake and funeral. I am sure that it meant a lot to his family. This death and vandalism is certainly maddening."

"But we don't want to start off on the wrong foot and get a bad reputation. We must let the police handle these matters. Chief Bratton has assured me that the entire Boston police force is investigating and has been instructed to watch the backs of cab drivers during this time of high-strung feelings."

"Look, let's stay out of the headlines for the wrong reasons. Let's continue to do a good job and provide good service to Boston. Next month, when the vote is complete, Boston's public will appreciate us keeping this process on the high road and will hopefully understand our plight and back our position.

"Conversely, I can assure that if you take this matter into your hands and into the gutter, the people of Boston will get a negative opinion of us and most likely side against us. So let's keep our cool. Let's let the police handle these matters, and let's stay on the high road."

"Now, let me hear you. All right?"

"Yea."

"Louder!"

"Yea!"

"Are you all on board?"

"Yea!!"

"Are we all staying on the high road?"

"Yea… "

"Great!"

"Now, keep that registration going. While you are waiting, feel free to grab a cup of coffee in the back of the room and take a minute to say high to your fellow drivers. Even though you may work for a different cab company, you will all be union brothers when the vote to organize is final."

"Once the voting results are complete it must be presented to the district court judge where it is reviewed for proper procedure and structure. If that condition is met, it is accepted as legally binding and put on permanent record at the courthouse. Our legal counsel will be certain to have this formal legal process started the day after the vote is taken, and completed as soon as possible."

"Gentlemen, once you have completed your registration, you are free to go. I look forward to seeing all of you on April 19th. Oh yea, and let's have a round of applause for the electrical workers union. They have generously allowed us the use of their hall and they sprung for that great coffee!"

The room explodes in applause.

The electrical steward, Bernie Martin, comes out from the bar area to the side and gives the gathering a wave and a nod. Then he retreats back into the bar.

Harry just smiles at Bernie and then shakes his head a little as Bernie turns toward the bar. He realizes that the Bernie Martin lifestyle is commonplace across the country in the union trade lifestyle… put in a hard days work, toss a few back with the boys, then get up the next day and do it all over again.

It is also universal that they don't want for more. A simple daily routine, ending each day with a simple beverage reward or two and maybe a ballgame on the TV is all they ask. Ok, maybe a winning lottery ticket too! Soon, Bernie will head home, hit the hay, and do it all again tomorrow.

By now the hall is nearly empty. The last few drivers sign the registration, and the stewards return their registration pads to Harry. Harry gathers up registration pads and other materials, packs them in his briefcase, and turns to Melio.

"Tonight, we had a very good meeting, Melio." "Now I'm hungry and I am tired. Can you get me back to my hotel?"

Melio smiles and says, "You ran a great show tonight, Harry. Let's go."

The two head back to the Bostonian.

Harry heads in, orders room service and calls it a day.

Melio pulls away from the hotel and drives into the Boston night, knowing he'll be back here in the morning to take Harry to meet with the State Senate Leader, Billy Bulger.

9:00 Wednesday morning

Melio roles up to the front entrance of the Bostonian Hotel. Harry is ready and waiting. He is dressed respectfully in a dark business suit. His tie knot is drawn tightly around his neck. Harry wants to his convey his respect to the President of the State Senate.

They quickly make the short ride to the front steps of the State Capital.

"Thanks Melio." "I'll call you if I need a ride after the meeting."

He jumps out of the cab and quickly ascends the substantial stairway rising to the State Capital front door. Inside the door Harry approaches the information officer.

"Good morning," Harry says in an engaging manner.

The officer nods in acknowledgement.

"I'm here to meet with Senator Bulger."

The officer waves his arm toward a bank of elevators and replies, "Third floor, then go left. The Senator's office is at the end of that hall."

Harry gives a quick wave of thanks and heads to the elevator. Both houses are in session today, making the Capital building is alive with activity.

Harry makes his way onto a crowded elevator, and the big steel and brass box ascends slowly to the third floor. As the door slides open, Harry heads to the left and proceeds directly to the office at the end of the hall.

Inside, the receptionist asks, "how can I help you, sir?"

"I'm Harry Sharpstone, and I have a 9:30 appointment with Senator Bulger."

"Yes, Mr. Sharpstone. Senator Bulger is expecting you. You may head right in."

The receptionist looks toward the Senator's office door. Harry smiles at the receptionist.

"Thank you Miss."

Then he proceeds into the Senator's office.

"Good morning Mr. Sharpstone."

Senator Bulger stands up from his desk and extends his hand to greet Harry.

"Good morning, Senator Bulger."

Then, a well-dressed man, with thinning white hair man stands up turns and smiles. Harry pauses briefly. He was not expecting anyone else at the meeting. Harry shakes Senator Bulger's hand, and then turns to greet the other man present.

"Good morning, Congressman Moakley. This is a pleasant surprise."

The three men sit down. A clerk has entered in the office and proceeds to serve them coffee.

Congressman Joseph Moakley was born in Boston in 1927. He was raised in South Boston. He served in the United States Navy during World War II. After the war, he attended the University of Miami in Coral Gables, Florida. He graduated from Suffolk University Law School, right behind the State Capitol, in 1956. He was a Boston City Councilman from 1971 to 1973.

In 1972, Joe ran for Congress in the 9th District, that includes a large share of Boston and South Boston, as well as many South Shore communities, as an Independent. The incumbent was Democrat Louse Day Hicks. Joe defeated her by 3400 votes. After being elected, Joe declared his party affiliation to be Democrat. Joe was reelected 14 times.

He served as Majority Whip under Speaker of the House Tip O'Neill, who was also a Massachusetts Congressman. They were close friends and political allies. Joe was also chairman of the powerful House Committee on Rules.

Congressman Moakley leads into the conversation.

"Harry, when I heard of your meeting this morning, I just wanted to take this opportunity to personally thank you for all of the support shown by you and the members of the Teamsters during my election campaigns."

"Thank you Congressman Moakley. However, you have been such a great supporter of the Teamsters over the years that the guys are always eager to rally support for your reelection."

"Harry", says Senator Bulger, "when Congressman Moakley asked me to save a seat for you at the Saint Patrick's Day breakfast, I knew that you must have special meaning to him. I have always supported organized labor. I surmised that you must be in town for a significant reason. If your efforts require my assistance then by all means give me a call."

Harry is taken by the warm reception and the offer of assistance.

"Thank you, Senator Bulger. I appreciate your offer. My purpose here is rather substantial. I have been sent to organize the cab drivers."

"Bravo!" exclaims Senator Bulger. "I am all for blue collar workers organizing to better their quality of life. When will the vote take place?"

"We are scheduled for the vote on April 19th"

"Excellent, you have really worked quickly. However, I understand that strong acts of opposition are already taking place."

"That's right, Senator. Unfortunately, the weeks preceding any vote to organize always stir up passion and anxiety on both sides of the issue. I was hoping that you might know of the source of this recent violence."

"Well Harry, typically I'm not privy to those who commit such violent acts. I understand that Chief Bratton has Boston's finest on high alert. He's a good man. I'm confident that he will solve these crimes swiftly."

"Thank you Senator Bulger. I know you are a busy man. Are there any other questions that I can answer for you or the Congressman?"

Senator Bulger replies, "Actually the only question I have is what else can I do for you today?"

"Well, I do have one other concern."

"What is that, Harry?"

"The judicial validation of the Union vote can sometimes contain last minute opposition."

"I see" says Senator Bulger, "Well, I'm confident that the judicial validation will go smoothly."

The thought conveyed was clear without another word. Harry gets a sense that he can rely on a guardian angel in the form of Senator Bulger to make sure that the judicial validation of the union vote is a smooth and successful process.

"Thank you, Senator Bulger. It is an honor to meet you, Congressman Moakley. Now, I'll let you two men return to your important business at hand."

Senator Bulger responds, "Thank you for stopping in Mr. Sharpstone. Have a great day."

Harry shakes the two men's hands and turns toward the door. He heads toward the elevators and then down to the main entrance.

As Harry steps outside, he pauses to admire the view of Boston Common. He notices the good people of Boston going about their business and enjoying the park. The sun is beaming. The sky is clear. It is simply a beautiful Spring day in Boston.

Harry has an open schedule for the rest of the day. He decides to take a walking tour and take in the sights, sounds, and smells, while noting the history and culture of this great city.

Upon descending the steps of the State Capitol, Harry turns left on Beacon Street and passes by the small shops on Beacon Hill. He turns left on Tremont Street, and then crosses over onto City Hall Plaza. Harry stops to process the structure in front him, Boston City Hall.

Perhaps the best description of this building is: a dysfunctional contemporary design featuring an assortment of commercial construction materials dominated by concrete, glass and steel, poorly arranged into a multi-story structure highlighted by leaks, cracks, and malfunctioning equipment with an overall look that is thoroughly displeasing to the human eye. Amazingly, the architect, who shall remain nameless, has created a government building that truly depicts government.

Harry shakes his head and smiles while taking in this sight. He strolls across the plaza and down the stairs. Then he crosses Congress

Street and proceeds up North Street, between the rear delivery doors to Faneuil Hall on the right, and the Union Oyster House and the Purple Shamrock on the left.

Just ahead is the entrance to the Bostonian Hotel.

Suddenly, a dark sedan pulls up next to Harry. Three thugs jump out and proceed to beat Harry with fists and clubs. Instantly, the undercover police parked in front of the Bostonian react. They swiftly move in, block the dark sedan with their car and confront the thugs. Two other cruisers move in, and the entire group of batterers is apprehended.

"Are you OK, Mr. Sharpstone?" asks one of the officers as he helps Harry up. Harry pauses. One of his batterers yells, "leave town, teamster" as he is being loaded into a cruiser.

"Get them out of here. Book them and hold them", the officer shouts back. "Get a tow truck", he orders. "I want this car to have a complete search. I want this registration and ownership traced."

Harry has steadied himself and regained his composure. He examines himself for injuries and discovers that he has a bloody lip and a large welt on top of his head. At this point, they are nearly in front of the Bostonian Hotel. The officer grabs a cold pack and a gauze pad from his first aid kit. Harry applies them to his wounds. His suit is torn in several locations.

"Thank you, officers. You saved my skin. I think I will be all right", Harry mutters.

He is still somewhat dazed. Suddenly, everything looks blurry to Harry. He faints and collapses to the ground. Harry is unconscious. The attending officer calls for an ambulance, and Harry is taken to Massachusetts General Hospital.

When Harry resumes consciousness, he finds himself lying in a hospital bed. After a few minutes a nurse comes in to take his vital signs. "Mr. Sharpstone," the nurse explains, "you have suffered a concussion. You have been admitted to Mass General Hospital for observation. I suggest that you stay in bed for now, as you will probably pass out and fall again if you stand up."

Harry has a thermometer in his mouth, an intravenous needle in his left arm, and a blood pressure cuff on his right arm. Realizing that he is not going anywhere, he settles back into his pillow. Harry dozes off.

About 2:00 P.M., Harry awakens to find the police officer who assisted him, and his partner, standing beside his bed. Harry focuses on them, and pauses. Then Harry grabs the cup next to his bed and takes a drink.

"Gentlemen, it's nice to see you again," Harry starts in. "What can I do for you?"

"Mr. Sharpstone, we have the three men who beat you in custody. They will probably be arraigned in the morning."

"That's great," Harry responds.

"Would you like to give a statement at this time?" asks the officer.

"I really have nothing to say. I was jumped and beaten up. It happened so quick that I have no idea who those guys were. Thank goodness you guys were tailing me. I'm sure that you had a better view than I did."

"Do you have any idea who any of these men are, Mr. Sharpstone?" asks the Police Officer.

"No, I don't. Do you?" Harry responds.

"Mr. Sharpstone, one of the thugs is named Angelo Ragatini. Is that name familiar to you?"

"No, officer. I can't say it is. Should it be?"

"Well, our investigation is ongoing. However, Mr. Ragatini's father and uncle own more than seventy Boston taxi medallions."

"Wow. I see. Well, it sounds like you are onto something. Is there anything else?"

"Yes there is."

"Go ahead. "I can't stand the suspense."

"We found three ice picks in the trunk of the car."

"Wow," Harry says again. "I see. Dare I ask if there is anything else?"

"Yes, Mr. Sharpstone, there is… "

"Go on… "

"We also found a detonator, wiring, and explosives in the trunk of the car."

"Wow!" Harry yells, "Jackpot! That is great work, gentlemen. Ouch! I'm sorry, my head is throbbing."

A nurse hurries in with pain pills. "Here Mr. Sharpstone, take these for the pain." Harry takes the pills and settles down.

"Thank you nurse. Thank you officers. You are doing a great job. Now I need some rest."

The police officers leave.

"Get some rest, Mr. Sharpstone," says the nurse, "and keep that cold compress on your head."

The nurse adjusts the cold compress and leaves.

Moments later, Harry digs his cell phone out of the night stand and calls Attorney Martin.

"Hello, Tim Martin."

"Hello Tim, its Harry Sharpstone."

"Hi Harry, how was your meeting with Senator Bulger?"

"That meeting went very well. However, I decided to walk back to the hotel and that did not end well."

"Really? What happened?"

"Well, I was approaching the hotel when suddenly I was jumped and beat up."

"My goodness. Where are you now?"

"I've been admitted to Mass General Hospital. Can you stop by when you get a chance? I have a lot of details to go over."

"Sure, Harry, I'll be by around 6:00 P.M. In the meantime, hang up the phone and get some rest."

"Thanks Tim, I'll see you then."

Harry hangs up, rolls over and dozes off.

It is now about 6:00 P.M. Harry is stirring. He senses someone walking in the room. It's Tim Martin. A nurse enters the room, checks Harry vital signs and changes his intravenous bottle. Harry has a thermometer in his mouth and a blood pressure cuff on. He looks toward Tim and raises his index finger as if to ask for one minute. They nod to each other.

"Harry you need to continue to rest", orders the nurse. "There is a dinner tray here. The doctor will be in around 11:00 tomorrow morning to examine you. Until then keep the cold compress in place and get some rest. Let me know if you need more ice for that compress."

Harry responds, "Thank you nurse."

She leaves the room. Harry turns to Tim.

"Have a seat. Care for some dinner?"

Tim smiles. "No thanks. You go ahead."

"Well Tim, I have had a very productive day!"

"I've got to here this."

"Yea, I met Senator Bulger and Congressman Moakley this morning for coffee at the State House. After that meeting, I decided to Walk back to the Bostonian. I was about fifty yards from the Bostonian when I was jumped and clubbed. Thank goodness the police have been tailing me all week. They were right on the spot. They grabbed the thugs and arrested them. Then I passed out. When I came to, I was here."

"I see," says Tim. "Is that it?"

"No. It gets better!"

"I see. Go on."

"Well, the police were here when I came to. They told me that the leader of the thugs was Angelo Ragatini. Do you know him?"

"Can't say I do," says Tim. "Who is he?"

"Well, apparently his father and his uncle have over seventy Boston Taxi cab medallions. Tim, those are worth about $275,000 a piece! These guys have some serious wealth, and a strong vested interest in seeing the union effort fail."

"Wow," exclaims Tim. "Is there anything else?"

"Oh yea," Harry continues. "It gets better. The police searched the trunk of their car. Tim, they hit the jackpot. Inside the trunk they found three ice picks. Then they found a detonator, wiring, and explosives. I think these guys may have slashed those tires at the wake and set the bomb that killed Barry. But I know how this can go. Are they actually the ones or did someone else put that stuff in the trunk. But boy, we certainly know the general direction now. Tim, they are going to be arraigned in the morning. Could you cover that whole mess for me?"

"Harry, I already have plans to be at the courthouse in the morning. I'll take care of it. Harry, here is my contract for this representation."

Harry just takes the contract turns to the last page and signs. "I'm sure it is all in order as we discussed. Thank you Tim." Harry returns the contract.

"Tim, I'll probably be back at the Bostonian tomorrow afternoon. I'll give you a call. It's amazing how a simple beating can solve so many questions."

The two men laugh.

"You are tough, Harry. I'll take care of these legal issues. Eat your dinner. Get some rest. I'll talk to you tomorrow afternoon."

Tim leaves.

Harry eats his bologna and cheese sandwich, washes it down with ginger ale and then onto desert, cherry flavored Jello!

As Harry eats his dinner he wonders, are they trying to help me get better or are they trying to kill me with this food? He puts on the TV, flips through the channels and slowly drifts off to sleep.

Harry wakes up several times during the night. He maintains the cold compress. The nurses stop in several times to check his intravenous bottle and his vital signs. The night passes uneventfully.

VIII

Seven A.M.

Harry wakes up. There is still some pain from the contusion on his head. Harry grabs a mirror and checks the damage. The swelling is reduced considerably. There is a purplish colored reminder on his head. The other minor cuts and contusions are now incidental.

Breakfast rolls in. Scrambled eggs, English muffin, coffee and cranberry juice are served. After breakfast Harry goes through the sponge bath routine. The nurse comes in checks his vital signs and disconnects his I.V. hookup.

"How are you feeling today, Harry?"

"Much better thank you."

"Great. The doctor will be here in about one hour to see you. In the meantime stay in bed and maintain the cold compress."

She leaves. Harry obeys his orders. About one hour later the doctor arrives.

"Good morning, Harry."

"Hi, Doc."

The doctor gives Harry an examination, looking into his eyes with his light and asking questions.

"Do, you feel any dizziness?"

"No."

"How does that welt feel?"

"It's still a little sore but not bad."

"I see. Well, you certainly look a lot better. Let's get you up and see how you do."

Harry stands up a little wobbly but steadies himself right away.

"Very good, now let me see you walk up to the nurses station and back."

Harry accomplishes the walk with ease.

"OK Harry, I'm going to discharge you. Keep your activity low for two or three days. If you experience dizziness, vomiting or blackouts get back to the hospital right away. That's it. Any questions?"

"Yea Doc, just one. Am I clear to fly tomorrow afternoon?"

"Well, as long as you have none of those symptoms you should be good to go by then. Good luck Harry."

"Thanks, Doc."

A nurse comes in with Harry's clothes. Harry gets dressed and calls Melio.

"Hi Melio, it's Harry."

"Hi Harry, how was your walk yesterday?"

"Melio, it was great right up to the point when I got jumped by three thugs."

"What? Are you all right? What happened?"

"Melio, I'm all right now. Can you pick me up at Mass General Hospital? I'm being discharged. I'll tell you all the details when we get out of here."

"Sure Harry, I'll be right there."

Harry hangs up. A nurse comes into the room with a wheelchair.

"What's this?" asks Harry.

"It's your ride to the front door. Now climb aboard and off we go."

"I don't need a wheelchair."

"You don't get discharged without one, Harry. Now sit down and let's go."

Harry gives in. He sits down and off they go. By the time they reach the front door, Melio has arrived and is waiting.

The nurse wheels Harry to the door of Melio's cab. "OK, Mr. Sharpstone, now be careful. Don't bump your head and good luck to you."

Harry stands up and puts himself in the cab.

"Thank you for the great care. You are truly a dedicated bunch."

Harry closes the door and Melio pulls away.

"OK, Harry. Unload. What happened?"

"Well, the assault and battery was nothing special. As a matter of fact it was pretty routine. The assault combined with the instant police response seems a little too perfect."

"Harry, What are you talking about? You're losing me."

"Sorry about that Melio. I got ahead of myself. Do you have time for coffee?"

"Sure thing. Dunk'n Donuts is just around the corner."

They pull into the coffee shop, get their orders and sit down.

"OK, Melio. Here goes. I walked toward Fanueil Hall and then up North Street toward the Bostonian. I was about fifty yards from the hotel when these three thugs pulled up in a black sedan, jumped out, and proceeded to issue me a beating. They got in a few good shots and the police were on top of the scene like a laser shot. It was just too good. Then I passed out on the sidewalk and woke up in that bed at Mass General."

"I see, " says Melio.

"Melio, this gets weird. When I woke up the police who have been tailing us all over Boston are standing next to my bed. Their interrogation of me was lame. It was like they already knew all that they need to know."

"I see."

"But Melio, now it got really weird. They started sharing information as if they had been instructed to do so."

"What do you mean Harry?"

"You know how the police never share information from their investigation, well these guys were singing like a church choir."

"No kidd'n, what did they say?"

"First they told me that the lead thug is a guy named Angelo Ragatini."

"No!" exclaims Melio.

"Do you know him?"

"Yea, Harry, he's a spoiled brat from Charlestown. His Dad Bruno and his uncle Mario own a lot of medallions. They're big!"

"That's what I heard, Melio. But there's more."

"More? What else?"

"Apparently the search of the car revealed three ice picks in the trunk along with a detonator, wiring, and explosives."

Melio is stunned.

"Do you mean that these guys are on the hook for knocking off Barry and blowing out all those tires?"

"Well, Melio, the police still have to connect those contents of that closed trunk to the guys who beat me up but that shouldn't be too difficult. And who owns that car? Why are the police so talkative? I'm not convinced that this is all that it seems. Why would these guys jump me mid day in broad daylight? How could they miss that unmarked cruiser less than fifty yards down the road? Someone could have set them up with that car with all of the evidence in the trunk and then sent them along to bust me up and get themselves arrested."

"Wow Harry" Melio blurts out. "This is big. This is crazy. This whole thing is confusing."

"Melio, you have got to keep this quiet for now. If this gets out the cabbies could rush to judgment, revolt in the wrong direction, and create incidents that may hurt the integrity needed for the union organization. Let me think about this. Tim Martin is covering the arraignment action at the courthouse today. I'll try to figure this out tonight after I talk to Tim. Tomorrow I promised a news conference out front of the Bostonian at 11:00 A.M. Then I have a 2:00 flight back to Chicago. So let's head back to the Bostonian and then I'll let you go.

"I will need one more ride over to Logan Airport tomorrow right after the news conference and then I'll leave you alone for a while, I promise."

The two get up and head out to the cab.

"Harry, don't mention it. I haven't had this much excitement in years. It's good for the old ticker."

"Melio, keep your helmet on and your safety belt fastened, 'cause it ain't over by a long shot. I think we are in for a wild ride."

Harry heads into the Hotel, and up to his room. He smiles at his bed, flops on it, and dozes off. Harry awakes to his cell phone ringing away. He sits up and grabs it.

"Hello."

"Harry, it's Tim Martin. It sounds like I woke you up."

"That's Ok Tim. How did it go at the court house?"

"It was a long day. Angelo Ragatini and his two accomplices were only arraigned on assault and battery charges today. They all plead not guilty to the charges. The DA did a good job presenting. Counsel for Angelo Ragatini and the boys were really tap dancing. But the judge was having none of it. Bail was set rather high at $50,000 a piece."

"What about the other evidence?" Harry blasts back. "What about some vandalism and murder charges?"

"Harry, I talked it over with the District Attorney. He says that they want to complete their investigation a little further before they roll out the big charges. He also wants to see who posts that high bail for these guys and see where their trail leads."

"Gotcha, Tim."

"Anyway, Angelo Ragatini is the only significant one of the bunch. The other two are simply low-life thugs for hire. My strong advice at this point is keep quiet on this issue and let it play itself out."

"Aw, shoot!" Harry exclaims.

"What's wrong?"

"I just filled Melio in on all of the details."

"Harry, give me Melio's number and I'll emphasize to him the need to keep this quiet for now."

"Thanks Tim, now I've got one more issue before I leave town."

"When are you leaving?"

"My flight leaves at 2:00 P.M tomorrow. I promised the press that I would talk to them at 11:00 A.M. out front of the Bostonian."

"That's not a good idea Harry."

"I know Tim, but they ambushed me at the police station a few days ago. I promised that I would give the some time on Friday if they left me alone until then."

"I see."

"Yea, I know, they can be tough. So why don't you meet me out front tomorrow at 11:00 and jab me in the side if I need to change direction or create a verbal swerve."

"I'll be there Harry. Now get some rest."

"Thanks again Tim."

"Harry, you're welcome, besides, if no one is mixing it up then I don't have a paycheck."

"How true Tim, how true."

Harry hangs up the phone. He spends the evening resting, packing and preparing his thoughts for the press conference.

Friday Morning

March 23rd, 10:45 A.M. Harry heads down to the front desk to check out. Along the way he recaps his remarks for the press and prepares mentally for the rapid flurry of questions expected to follow. He reaches the front desk.

"I'm Harry Sharpstone, and I'm checking out."

"Ah, yes, Mr. Sharpstone. Here is your room statement for your stay. I certainly hope that you enjoyed your visit to Boston."

Harry reviews his bill, and makes payment.

"Thank you. This trip has certainly been memorable. I will be returning soon. My office will contact the hotel for reservations when my plans are finalized."

"Very good Mr. Sharpstone. Thank you for staying at the Bostonian Hotel."

Harry turns and heads through the front door. Melio is waiting there and takes Harry's suitcase to his cab. Out front there is a band of microphones set up by the press for Harry's statement and responses. Harry stops in front of the microphones and pauses while he views the gathering of reporters in front of him. Cameras click. Attorney Tim Martin takes his post next to Harry at the microphone.

"Thanks again, Tim." Harry says in a low tone. "Look Tim, right after this I am going to make a quick exit, so I'm saying goodbye now and I'll see you in April. Please keep me informed on the court proceedings and any further details for April."

They shake hands. Harry pulls his notes from his suit vest pocket. He quickly looks down at them. Then he looks up at the gathering and delivers his address.

"Good morning. I am Harry Sharpstone. I am employed as an organizer with the Teamsters Union of Chicago, Illinois. I have been here in Boston at the urging of the cab drivers of Boston to assist in organizing the group into a trade association for the purpose of alleviating their frustrations as a disorganized group with common industry and employment problems. Cab drivers have been enduring unsafe work conditions and an income level that cannot support the cost of living in greater Boston.

"The recent violent murder of cab driver Barry Blumberg from Charlestown is evidence of the heightened dangerous circumstances existing here in Boston. After many years of struggles and frustrations in the areas of safety and compensation cab drivers have decided that new action is needed to address these problems.

"I applaud this loosely organized brotherhood of cab drivers for examining union formation as a civilized and proper direction addressing these problems in common in a proper format. They have agreed to have an election to adopt union organization. If adopted, all Boston cab drivers would be required to belong to this soon-to-be-formed union as a condition or their employment. The election is scheduled to take place on Thursday, April 19th.

"I am impressed by the restraint and civility of Greater Boston's cab drivers to accept this process in order to achieve well-deserved redress of their issues. The people of Greater Boston should take note of their cab driver's hard work and dedication to their service to the city's transportation needs while enduring their difficult working circumstances. Thank you. And now I will take a few questions."

The group of reporters immediately start shouting questions toward Harry. Harry points to a reporter and says, "Yes sir, what is your question."

"Mr. Sharpstone, what can you tell us about the explosion of the executive car that was en route to pick you up?"

Harry pauses and begins "That act of violence which killed Barry Blumberg was quite unfortunate. It was not an accident. I suspect that my presence here touched a nerve with someone. My delayed arrival probably saved my life. I've got the message. However, this violent act only served to inspire me to move forward with this organizing effort. Chief Bratton and The City of Boston Police are working on the case. I am confident that they will resolve the matter. Let's leave it at that. Next question. Yes, you sir."

"Thank you. Where will this election take place and who is running the election locally?"

"OK," says Harry, "It's the old two-for-one double question." The reporters laugh. "For the sake of safety, the election location is known only to the Cab Drivers for now. Just prior to the election the polling location and interim local leaders will be announced to the public."

"Final question." says Harry, "Yes sir. Go ahead."

"Thank you. The bruise on your forehead appears quite serious and quite recent. Was there another violent act sustained by you recently, relative to this Union Organization?"

"Apparently so, but I was rendered unconscious so I really don't have any details to share. I imagine that the police report will provide more details than I can. Thank you very much, gentlemen. I'll see you after the election on April 19th."

Harry, quickly moves toward Melio's awaiting cab and hops in. As the cab moves around the courtyard, Harry notices an unmarked police cruiser dispatched to watch the event. Harry gives them a friendly wave good bye and they head for the airport without further incident.

Monday, March 26th

arry's back at the Teamster's headquarters in Chicago. It's a cold gray winter day. Still, Harry is glad to be back at the home base. The assignment in Boston has been tumultuous. Tonight will be different. Tonight Mayor Dailey is having a black-tie fundraiser. The teamsters have always been in the Mayor Dailey camp. Harry has been seated with some of Chicago's political newcomers. Strong political ties are the lifeblood of labor unions.

Harry shows up at the dinner via yellow cab. He believes in taking every opportunity to support his cause. He walks into the dinner gathering and waits in the receiving line. Harry greets the mayor.

"Mayor Dailey, it's an honor to be included in this gathering this evening."

"Why thank you Harry."

Harry slips the mayor a campaign donation check as they shake hands.

"Ah yes, thank you very much, Harry. I understand that you have been busy broadening the base in Boston."

"Well put, mayor. As usual, nothing gets by you."

"Harry, If I can make a call to help with that Boston effort just let me know."

"Thank you, Mayor. I'll certainly keep that in mind."

"Great. By the way, I've put you at a table with some political rising stars in Chicago politics. This group looks like they will go to the top of leadership quickly. Enjoy the evening Harry."

"Thank you Mayor. I certainly will."

Harry proceeds to his table. Thank goodness for the name cards on the table. These are all newcomers. Harry approaches his seat, and breaks the ice with the group. "Good evening, I'm Harry Sharpstone with the Teamsters Union."

"Well, good evening Harry, I'm State Senator Barack Obama, and this is my wife, Michelle. Let me introduce the rest of our table. This is Congressman Rod Blagojevich, and his wife Patricia, and next to him is Congressional advisor Rahm Emanuel and his wife, Amy."

"Well, It is certainly a pleasure to meet all of you. I know that it is not easy to break into politics in Chicago. Do you three gentlemen happen to have a secret to your political success?"

"Come on Harry," Rahm Emanuel responds, "You know if we share our secret with you we might have to kill you!" The group at the table starts to laugh. "Actually, Harry," says Rahm, "The secret for me is to never waste a good crisis."

Harry responds, "That's interesting, Rahm. I'll be sure to remember that: 'Never waste a good crisis'."

"Well Harry," exclaims Barack Obama, my secret is my lovely wife, Michelle. She is a great partner in every way."

"That's a great answer." Harry responds. "Gentlemen, please let me know if there is any way the teamsters can help as you move forward in your political careers. Oh, yea, and just don't forget about me when one of you takes over the White House." The entire table breaks out in laughter.

"That was a good one." Remarks Blagojevich. "Politics is a funny business. One minute you're headed for the White house and the next you're in handcuffs going off to jail. Harry, what I want to know is will you remember us when one of us gets lead off to jail!" The table breaks out in a roar of laughter.

"Well, Congressman," responds Harry, "it all depends on what you are going in for!" The table laughter continues. "Now, let's get a round of drinks for the table. It's on me."

Senator Obama offers to give Harry a hand. The two men head toward the bar.

Harry has no idea just how valuable tonight's new introductions might be in the future of politics and organized labor. But Harry understands that you always make a strong, memorable introduction, because you never know which introduction will prove to be valuable in the future.

Harry and Senator Obama make their way over to the bar. They put in the drink order for the table.

Senator Obama speaks in a low private tone to Harry. "Harry, I have mirrored your skills as a union organizer in my efforts as a community organizer."

"That is quite flattering, Senator."

"Well, you organize blue-collar workers into a collective bargaining group which creates immediate bargaining power for the group. Similarly, I organize those on welfare and unemployment and other government assistance into a group who, by virtue of the strength of their collective voting block, can influence the direction of expansion of their government benefits."

"Well, Senator, that is quite an interesting observation. Good luck with your efforts. It will be interesting to see how it all is received and develops on the national scene. I hope I am not too presumptuous. You are planning to go nationally aren't you?"

"Well, Harry, with the energy from your positive perspective, I think I will."

Just then, the two men are approached by another Illinois politician. Senator Obama greets the new arrival. "Well, hello there, brother Jesse."

Harry joins in. "Congressman Jackson. It's good to see you again."

Congressman Jesse Jackson replies. "Barry, and Harry, now there's a pair of Chicago's finest. Nice to see you gentlemen."

Harry asks "Can I by you a drink Congressman?"

"Thanks, Harry. I'll have a Budweiser."

"Of course," replies Harry, "what else would the owner of a Budweiser distributorship drink?" The three men break out in laughter.

"Anyway, thank you, Congressman, for being such a cooperative owner when it comes to our union negotiations."

"Well, Harry, let's not forget, your son Gregory is our shop steward and he is a chip off the old block. It would be foolish of me to become adversarial with a shop that runs as smoothly and profitably as ours. There is enough success to go around for everyone and, by the way, cooperation goes both ways. Thank you for the fine job that you, your son Gregory, and the union members do that keeps my distributorship number one. And, oh yea, thanks for the beer."

The three men return to their seats as dinner is served and Mayor Dailey is about to speak.

After dinner and the speech the party mode kicks in. Harry decides to call it a night. After all, it is a Monday night and he has a Tuesday morning meeting with Teamsters President, James Hoffa.

Harry reflects on his conversation with Congressman Jackson and it has him thinking about his son Gregory and his personal past. Harry is proud of his son's success as a Budweiser delivery driver and rising member in the Teamster's Union. He decides he will give him a call and see if they can get together for dinner later this week.

Harry married his high school sweetheart, Jill Paduka, when he returned from Vietnam, where he had been wounded in a grenade explosion. He struggled through business school at the University of Illinois using his veteran's benefits. Gregory was born while Harry was completing his final year of college.

Harry went right into office equipment sales after graduation. He needed to start making a paycheck right away to support his young family.

Harry and Jill divorced when Gregory was just six years old. Harry was not doing well as a sales rep. The stress of Harry's unhappiness at work was reflected in his poor earnings, which certainly contributed to the failing of his marriage. When Harry was bounced out of his marriage, he examined where his life was going.

The white-collar, corporate sales lifestyle was not working for him. In addition, working sixty hours a week kept him from his home life with his wife and young son. So, now that he had lost his marriage, he decided that he had to chuck the white-collar lifestyle, and he took a job loading beer trucks on the third shift.

Harry's new work schedule allowed him to have ample time to be a dad to his son. Meanwhile, at work the steady income and benefits agreed with Harry. He quickly worked his way up to route driver and eventually became shop steward. After work Harry attended young Gregory's football and basketball games and practices. He also was quite attentive to Gregory's homework and studies.

Harry was determined to be a success as a father. He believed that being an attentive parent and a strong role model with strong ethical and charitable values would go a long way to grooming his son's track in life. Harry is now convinced that his parenting plan worked.

Harry was selected to work for the Teamsters Union at the National level during Gregory's senior year of high school. Gregory, like his dad, went on to the University of Illinois business school. He loaded beer trucks as a summer job. He decided to stay with Budweiser after graduation. Gregory was married just last year. He continues to rise in the union leadership.

Gregory's mother passed away just two years ago from ovarian cancer. Harry had always remained close and cordial with Jill.

Tuesday, March 27th, 10:00 A.M. Harry promptly walks into the office of Teamsters President, James Hoffa.

"Good morning Harry, come on in and have a seat."

"Thank you, sir. It has been a while. It's nice to see you."

The two men sit down. Immediately, a staff person enters and serves both men coffee.

"Harry, from what I have seen and heard you are doing a great job in Boston. Can we, here in Chicago, provide any other assistance?"

"Well, Mr. Hoffa, thank you for the vote of confidence. Things are going well. There have been a few bumps and lumps along the road, but that is expected."

"Excellent. There is one other matter that I wish to bring up. Harry, our expansion is spreading you thin. So, in your travels, I want you to keep your eye open for candidates to become our next organizer."

"OK, sir."

"Does anyone come to mind at this time?"

"Why actually, yes there is one person that comes to mind."

"Who is that, Harry?"

"Tim Martin. I have hired him to be our legal counsel in the Boston organizing process. He has done a fine job thus far."

"Well, let's see how things play out in Boston. Then we can make a decision on him."

"That sounds like a good idea, Mr. Hoffa.

"Meanwhile, Harry, why don't you take a well-deserved vacation. And when you get back, you can return to Boston and see that election process through to its conclusion."

"Thank you, boss. I'm going deep-sea fishing, watch some baseball games, and maybe play some golf. I'll see you after the vote is complete in Boston."

The two men stand up and shake hands. Harry turns, leaves the office, and heads out on vacation.

Oh yes, thinks Harry, then there is Margaret. Margaret is Harry's latest girlfriend. She's always up for a vacation. I'll have to give her a call.

A refreshed Harry Sharpstone touches down at Logan Airport in Boston. Melio meets Harry at the arrival area.

"Harry, It's good to see you," pipes up Melio.

"Yea, it's good to see you again Melio. It's good to see you. Can we go somewhere and get a sandwich and catch up on the past couple of weeks?"

"Sure thing, Harry."

They hop in the cab and head for Kelly's Roast Beef, across from the beach in Revere at 410 Revere Beach Boulevard. On the way, Melio puts on the radio.

"AM 680 WRKO, Welcome to 'The Howie Carr Show', I am Howie Carr. As the listeners know I am usually dragging after the weekend. And today your tax returns are due. You can get to work and get that tax return done by midnight, but you might want to just file an extension and listen to this show because today is different. Today is a special day. I am just giddy with anticipation of tomorrow's criminal proceeding on the Ragatini thugs from the North End.

"I am excited with anticipation that these thugs are going to finally get the conviction and long sentences that are long over due. Do you here that, Judge? Long overdue. I understand that this is just the assault and battery charge for the beating, oh I'm sorry, 'alleged beating' that was administered to that union guy, Harry Sharpstone. But this will put them away long enough for the DA to put together the case for murder of local Charlestown cab driver Barry Blumberg?

"My paperboy juices haven't been flowing like this since FBI agent John Connolly was convicted for racketeering and being in cahoots with James 'Whitey' Bulger. OK, callers, let's work on two topics here this hour: Topic One is how long are these thugs going to get for their sentence, and Topic Two, where the heck is 'Whitey' Bulger hiding?"

Whitey Bulger is the#2 Most Wanted criminal in the world behind#1, Osama Bin Laden. Whitey is wanted for various gangster activities, including murder.

The remains of several of Whitey's alleged victims were found on the vacant lot owned by the firefighters union, across from Florian Hall, several years ago. Whitey Bulger is the older brother of former President of the State Senate, Billy Bulger. Billy has testified under oath before a US Senate investigative committee that he has no idea where his brother Whitey might be.

Whitey also had the good luck and good fortune to "purchase" a winning lottery ticket at his South Boston liquor store worth more than one million dollars. Coincidence? You decide.

He also had the good fortune to leave town and go underground just before the FBI was to place him under arrest. He remains at-large.

Melio and Harry arrive at Kelly's Roast Beef and head in. They order their sandwiches and drinks and take a table in an isolated corner.

"OK Melio, what has been going on the past couple of weeks?"

"Harry, there has been a lot of tension and penned-up frustration amongst the drivers. They can't wait to vote on Thursday."

"Actually, that's great Melio. We need their heightened focus for a strong vote of solidarity on Thursday. It sounds like they are ready.

"A good result from the vote will also relax their tension and satisfy their desire to unionize. This is a big deal. Have there been any incidents?"

"No Harry. Amazingly, the group has been on good behavior. They understand that a public display of their frustration may hurt their cause. They believe that their time is coming soon."

"Melio, you've done a great job for this cause. Put this in your pocket." Harry hands Melio an envelope.

"What's this?"

"Cab fare, Melio. Now, are we all set with the electrician union's hall for the voting?"

"Yea. Actually, your office has been great coordinating all of the details."

"Excellent. This is our business. We have to be good at this. Let's head for the hotel."

"Are we heading for the Bostonian?"

"No. Thanks for asking, Melio. This time I am staying at Le Meridien."

"Why the change Harry?"

"Well, the police and the thugs will expect me to show up at the Bostonian this week with the election at hand. Hopefully, I can avoid their watchful eyes for a couple of days by changing hotels."

Tuesday April 17th, 10:00 A.M., Boston District Court, across from City Hall Plaza, the Ragatini group are arraigned for the assault and battery inflicted on Harry Sharpstone. Prior to the trial the defense counsel and the District Attorney were engaged in heavy discussions and negotiations in a corner in the hallway. As the trial begins, the District Attorney asks if the lawyers may approach the bench. At the side bar, the District Attorney indicates that the accused are willing to plead guilty, in exchange for a thirty-day sentence.

The Judge glances over at Harry, who is sitting in the front row behind the DA's table. He then shakes his head and says "Mr. Sharpstone was jumped and beaten severely. This was not a random act. It was a vicious, premeditated act. Here is my offer. I'll agree to a two-and-a-half year sentence for a guilty plea. Otherwise, if we go to trial and they are found guilty, I will promise a minimum five-year sentence. Now, I am going to put this court in recess for ten minutes. When we resume, I hope we have reached a plea agreement. Now step back."

Loudly, the judge exclaims "This court stands in recess for ten minutes."

The Judge bangs the gavel. The court officer announces, "all rise." The judge gets up and leaves the courtroom.

The defendants are huddled at the table with their counsel. The reactions are of upset and frustration as the defense counsel reveals their options. At first there are shaking heads and the loud exclamations of "no way" and "I'm not doing that kind of time." The defense counsel continues to speak to them. He tells them that their chances of a "not guilty" finding at trial are highly unlikely, and in such a case they can expect a minimum sentence of five years. He strongly urges them to take the plea at two-and-a-half years and put this behind them. There is a long pause for thought. The group of thugs exchanges glances, and then collectively nod in agreement to plead guilty and accept the sentence offered.

Meanwhile, the DA leans in to talk with Harry.

"Harry, the Judge has a good handle on this case. He has offered a two-and-a-half year sentence in exchange for a guilty plea. This works to our favor, because we will have moved through the murder case of Barry Blumberg by that time and if convicted they will be put away for a long time. In the meantime, they will not get out before the completion of the murder trial.

"Harry, this saves you the uncomfortable need to testify. It also achieves certainty of a guilty sentence along with a rather firm sentence."

Harry barely needs to think about this one, even though it's not his decision anyway. Besides, this battery was nothing compared to what he experienced in Vietnam in hand-to-hand combat.

"Great job, Counselor." "Even though it is not my call, I am on board with this decision. I hope they plead out."

"All rise."

The judge returns to the courtroom.

"Please be seated. Defense counselor, would you like to make a statement or change of plea at this time?"

"Yes, Your Honor."

"Go ahead, Counselor."

"The defendants have decided to change their plea to guilty, and throw themselves on the mercy of the Court."

"I see. In light of this new position, the Court accepts the plea of guilty, and sentences the defendants to two-and-a-half years in jail. This sentence is to start immediately, with no chance of parole. Would the victim like to make a statement?"

"Yes, I would, your honor." Harry replies.

"Go right ahead, Mr. Sharpstone."

"Thank you, Your Honor." Harry pauses in thought, then starts. "You three miserable pieces of excrement fight like high-school girls in a pillow fight. Hopefully, two-and-a-half years is enough for you to learn how to make a fist and develop a muscle or two. In the meantime, don't drop the soap."

"Thank you, Mr. Sharpstone," acknowledges the judge. "This matter is closed."

"All rise."

The judge gets up and leaves the courtroom.

Harry smiles and chuckles, and as he leaves the courtroom, he is wondering, did State Senator Bulger make a phone call? Or maybe chief Bratton put in a word. Or maybe the judge just got it right. We may never know how this verdict truly came about, but it appears that today justice has been served.

Harry decides to walk back to Le Meridien Hotel. His cell phone rings as he descends the courthouse steps.

"Hello, this is Harry Sharpstone, who's this."

"Hello Harry, it's Chief Bratton. I trust things are going along OK as you approach your vote to unionize."

"As a matter of fact, things are going well, Chief Bratton. Thank you for asking."

"That's great Harry. Is the assault and battery trial on recess?"

"Actually, the trial is over, Chief. The defendants plead guilty and in so doing were sentenced to a two-and-a-half year sentence."

"Talk about swift justice. Why, Harry, that sounds great. Harry, with the tragic murder of Barry Blumstead, the incident at the funeral parlor, the assault and battery sustained by you, and the subsequent arrest of your assailants, tensions are heightened in the cab industries, and that translates to heightened tensions on the streets. Harry, I hope you will work with me to relieve this high tension."

"Chief Bratton, what can I do to help?"

"Thank you Harry. First of all, I would like to post a couple of officers at the union polling place on Thursday. I hope you can confirm where the polling will take place and at what time."

"Chief Bratton, the voting will take place at the electricians union hall from eight in the morning until eight in the evening. Thank you for offering the police presence."

"Your welcome Harry. Now, one more matter, in light of the battery issued to you and the court process today, will you permit us to have a squad car shadow you through your stay here this week?"

"I suppose that would be good idea. I am staying at Le Meridien Hotel."

"Thank you Harry."

"Chief, I have one question for you. In light of your unique situation where you issue the taxi medallions, is there any pressure being applied to you to apply pressure to me to back down and go away?"

The chief takes a long pause before answering.

"I'll be honest with you, Harry. There have been some calls of concern, and while they have not crossed the line into inappropriate conduct, they have brought me to heightened awareness. I am certainly standing in the middle here, and so I will function as the referee and provide the necessary law enforcement to allow this process to reach its own legal conclusion."

"That's fair enough, Chief. Thank you for your open response."

"Harry. There's one last thing. This conversation is just between us."

"You've got it, Chief."

"Thanks and goodbye for now, Harry."

"Goodbye chief."

Harry makes his way back to the Meridian. Parked out front already is an unmarked patrol car. Harry takes the rest of the day to double-check on the election details, such as ballots, candidates for shop steward, poll workers, and the release of final polling details for the cab drivers.

Harry's cell phone is ringing.

"Good morning, Harry Sharpstone."

"Harry, it's Melio."

"Good morning, Melio. What's up?"

"Well Harry, I guess you could say it was a wild night."

"How so, Melio?"

"Well, at about one o'clock in the morning, all hell broke loose. There was a racket outside of my place. Then I heard glass breaking, and there was a loud bright explosion. When I went to the window to check out this racket, I see my cab going up in a blazing ball of fire. Then gunfire broke out, and my windows were shot out."

"Are you OK, Melio?"

"Well, I took some glass shrapnel on my forehead, and a bullet grazed my left shoulder, but I'm OK. Boy, that bullet stung."

"Melio, did you get medical attention? Where are you now?"

"I just got released from the hospital. I spent the night at Mass General. One of my drivers is taking me home."

"Melio, swing by your house and get what you need for a few days. Then, get a communication blast out to the cab drivers. Let them know what happened, and that you are all right. But emphasize that voting on Thursday is the best retaliation, and that should be the only retaliation. Justice will prevail.

Then I want you to come down to the Meridian and check in. I'll call the front desk and reserve you a room. I will take care of the tab.

There is a Boston Police detail parked out front watching me. We might as well have them protect you during this tense time as well."

"Harry, I appreciate the offer, but I should be OK."

"Listen knucklehead. Someone just shot at you and landed a bullet within six inches of your heart. Get your butt down here and check in and then get some rest. Meanwhile, I'll get a glass company to your place, and a cleaning service to clean up. So, plan on staying here until Saturday. Let things cool down."

"You're right Harry. I'll be along."

"Great. Meanwhile, get that info blast out to the cab drivers, then get some rest. We have a big day tomorrow, and I want you at the voting poll with me."

"You bet, Harry, I wouldn't miss this vote, period."

"Melio, once you check in and get some rest, call the police and make sure that you give your statement."

"Harry, they met up with me at the hospital a couple of hours ago and that is all set."

"OK, Melio. I'll catch up with you after you get some rest. Leave a spare house key under your rear doormat for the workers I am sending over. They will lock the house and destroy the key when they are done."

"Thanks Harry."

"Catch you later, Melio."

Harry remembers what Rahm Emanuel mentioned to him at the dinner in Chicago: "Never waste a good crisis." He didn't quite understand him then. But he does now.

The rage to be felt by the cab drivers once they hear about this incident should certainly translate to a vote of support for the Union organization on Thursday.

Harry calls Chief Bratton.

"Hello, Chief Bratton, Harry Sharpstone here."

"Harry, I suppose you know about the incident at Melio's place."

"Yes, I do, Chief. Are there any suspects at this point?"

"Well, as you know, I don't comment on ongoing investigations. However, I have several officers investigating evidence and leads as we speak. Harry, I want to resolve this quickly, and nip a potential big problem in the bud."

"Melio is going to be close by my side for a few days. Please let your officers know. I hope they will watch his flank for a few days, along with mine."

"Thanks for that information, Harry. I'll be sure that our patrols, assigned to you and the upcoming union vote, are aware of Melio's presence."

"Great job, Chief. Thank you very much."

"Your welcome, Harry. And Harry, please pass along to the cab drivers that their restraint and professionalism is greatly appreciated by me."

"I'll do that, Chief. Thanks."

Harry and Melio arrive at the polling place, the Electricians Union Hall. There are about thirty to forty cab drivers already waiting for a chance to vote.

Bernie Martin is there from the Electricians Union. The hall is ready. In addition, he has provided an urn of coffee for the group. Tim Martin is also out front to meet Harry and Melio.

A uniformed police detail is in place. In addition, the patrol assigned to tail Harry is in the parking lot and watching the area.

Poll workers are inside and ready to go.

As Harry and Melio get out of the cab, the cab drivers notice Melio, and break out in a loud rousing cheer of "Meel-e-o, way to go." "We're with you Melio. Today we'll speak with our votes."

Harry is impressed. This voting block is solid with determination.

"Good morning gentlemen." Tim Martin pipes up. "It sure is a beautiful spring day here in Boston."

"Tim," Harry responds, "you and Bernie have done a great job getting this polling operation up and running."

The men go inside as the crowd assembled cheers. There is a strong positive vibe in the air. As they enter the hall, the poll workers turn their attention to them.

Harry addresses the group. "Has attorney Tim Martin informed you of your duties here today?"

The group answers in unison. "Yes Sir."

"Wow." Harry remarks. "I am impressed by this group. Thank you for your help. We will have donuts and sandwiches for you as the day progresses. Are there any last minute questions?"

The group murmurs in the negative.

"Great. Being seven-fifty-nine, let's take our places. The poll is about to open."

8:00 A.M. sharp. The polling doors open. The cab drivers file in. They are in a positive, spirited mood as they proceed in an orderly fashion though the voting process. After they vote, some of them stop in the side room for coffee, while others leave and go about their day. Within the first hour roughly seventy cab drivers have been in to vote.

The mood remains very upbeat all day. Cab drivers continue to arrive and vote in a constant stream. Harry and Melio remain at the voting hall all day long. Attorney Tim Martin directs them to an area where they can observe without being in violation of polling place laws. All voting takes place in proper fashion all day. Poll workers are relieved and nourished on a regular basis.

Finally, at 8:00 P.M. the poll is closed. The votes are tallied by the election officials. At 9:00 P.M. all the results have been tallied.

The media have gathered in a designated area and assembled a bank of microphones. The election officials head to the microphones and the head of the officials steps up to speak.

"Today we had 98 percent turnout of all known cab drivers in the city of Boston. The group posted a 96 percent vote in favor of union organization."

A loud cheer goes up at the polling place. The group gathered feels an unbelievable rush of joy and adulation. They realize that their work lives, pay level, and complete lifestyle are about to change for the better. They are now a collective bargaining group. They are now going to be able to lobby for access to the purchasing process of cab medallions. They will have a seat, a voice, and a vote at the Mayor's cab-fare rate-setting hearings, and the fare-splitting negotiations.

They will be able to purchase health insurance and other benefits through their newly formed union organization.

The news hits the airwaves and taxicab horns are heard all over the city of Boston. Boston has just become the first city in the entire United States of America to have an organized cab drivers union.

The bar opens at the Electrician's Union Hall and celebration begins. Cab drivers arrive from all over the city to join in the celebration. It continues long into the night. Harry and Tim have thought of everything. They have even arranged for sober drivers to make sure that everyone gets home safely.

10:00 A.M. Friday. Harry and Attorney Tim meet at the courthouse. Tim has prepared the necessary declarations in advance to file with the court. They head into the clerk's office and present the papers. The clerk glances at the filing and asks them to please wait. Harry and Tim look at each other with looks of concern. Tim responds, "of course." The clerk heads in the back with the paperwork.

Two minutes later he returns and says, "please come with me."

Harry and Tim follow the clerk. He leads them into Judge Sullivan's office. The Judge is reviewing the paperwork at his desk. The Judge looks up and says "Good morning gentlemen. Please have a seat. I should be done here in just a minute or two. Clerk Braithwaite, please wait here."

"Yes your honor" the clerk responds. He then remains standing next to the Judge's desk.

The Judge continues his review and eventually reaches the last page. This is the signature page. He looks up at Harry and Tim and exclaims, "everything appears to be in order."

He then proceeds to sign the documents and hands them to Clerk Braithwaite, stating, "Please take these documents and put them on record. Then return the originals to Attorney Martin."

"Yes sir," the clerk responds, as he takes the documents and leaves to put them on record.

"Gentlemen," the Judge pipes up, "that matter is complete." The Judge is now smiling at Tim and Harry and says, "Congratulations and good luck. Now get out of my office and stay out of trouble. Clerk Braithwaite will have your signed and recorded documents for you at the front desk."

The three men stand up and shake hands.

"Thank you your honor." Harry and Tim respond in unison.

Then they leave the office and head out to the front desk to retrieve their documents. The two men are in shock. They both know that this type of thing almost never goes smoothly like this. They are speechless. They mindlessly proceed together out the front door of the courthouse.

Suddenly, Harry's cell phone rings. "This is Harry."

"Ah, yes Mr. Sharpstone, it certainly is a beautiful day in Boston. I trust everything went well at the courthouse this morning."

"Why, why yes S-s-senator Bulger. Everything went just fine. Thank you." Harry stutters.

"Splendid, Mr. Sharpstone. I'm very sorry to hear about that terrible attack inflicted on Melio Rocco. My goodness. I hope justice is dealt to those responsible. By the way, a thank you is not necessary, however I certainly hope you can attend my 'time' in mid-December."

(A 'time' is a political fundraiser. Typically, those who attend pass along a campaign donation to the host in the receiving line. This practice is usually a sort of thanks for favors received or a future anticipated consideration.)

"I will be certain to be there, Senator Bulger, thank you for the invitation."

"It's my pleasure Mr. Sharpstone. I'll be sure to have you contacted with the details. In the meantime, congratulations and good fortune to you, and the newly organized cab drivers of Boston."

"Thank you very much, Senator Bulger, thank you very much."

The Senator has the last word: "Farewell Mr. Sharpstone, farewell."

Harry Looks at Attorney Martin. "Tim, you are not going to believe… "

Tim jumps in, "I heard Harry, I heard."

The two men head down the steps to a waiting cab and they are driven to Tim's office.

As the two travel back to Tim's office, they listen to the 12:00 news on the cab radio.

"This is Listo Fisher with the 12:00 O'clock news update… ..Two men were found slumped over in their car in Charlestown this morning.

They were both shot in the back of the head. According to sources, the two dead men were suspects in the assault and battery inflicted on cab driver Melio Rocco from Charlestown a few days ago."

Harry and Tim look at each other with looks of amazement.

"Tim, I sense an elevation in friction developing and a spreading base of interest and activity."

"I know what you mean by elevated friction, Harry, but what do you mean a spreading base of interest?"

"Well Tim, I can't quite put my finger on it, but who would be knocking off the guys that assaulted Melio? That's a pretty strong retaliation."

Tim is paused in thought. "Harry, you are right. Tensions and reactions are elevating, and the cast of participants seems to be spreading."

"Tim, it sounds like you have some local knowledge that I may be missing. Can you offer a little more?"

"Sure, Harry, but let's cover that at my office."

At the office they sit down at the desk.

"OK, Tim, what else do you know about the heightened tensions and actions?"

"Harry, do you remember when Senator Bulger called you on the phone, and hoped that those who battered Melio would get justice?"

"Sure Tim, what about it?"

"Well, he may have been eluding that he made a call to make sure that they received justice, and in this case, he meant street justice. You see, Harry, Senator Bulger has a brother in South Boston named Whitey. It is no secret that Whitey Bulger is the crime boss of South Boston. He is being investigated for many mob-style murders over the years, but has yet to be arrested."

"So Boston's political strong man and Boston's top mobster are actually brothers?"

"Exactly. And I'm guessing that Billy might have spoken with Whitey, and Whitey followed up with some street justice."

"Tim, I've lived with Chicago and it's corruption for years, but this one beats anything in Chicago. I actually just felt a chill up my back. I don't want that blood on my hands, and I do not want that execution tied back to this union organization. I need to set a tone. I need to let the public know that we are not tied to that mob-style hit. We do not endorse violence in any form, and particularly in a function such as union organizing."

"Well, Harry, your flight leaves in the morning. So how do you propose to get this message out?"

"Tim, I think I will call that talk show host, Howie Carr, and see if he will put me on for a minute."

"Harry, he is going to want to question you. He is a reporter. He could try to trip you up."

"Tim, I have been doing this for years. Something needs to be done now. I am going forward with this."

"Harry, this could be risky, but doing nothing is definitely risky. So I say, give it a go."

"Thanks Tim, I appreciate your advice. Now, I need to take this conversation in another direction. We have officially established a cab drivers' union here in Boston. Going forward, the union leadership needs to be in on rate negotiations with the Mayor, rate-split discussions with the cab company owners, and all other union management negotiations. I need someone that has a strong background in negotiation, mediation and arbitration to handle this new union chapter for the teamsters. I believe that you are the guy to take the reigns of the oversight of this operation. I need you Tim. I am offering you this position. What do you say?"

"Harry, I am ready to go." responds Tim.

"Tim, it is interesting that you put it that way, because I want to ask you to join me in Chicago next week. Union President Hoffa would like to meet you. I am leaving for Chicago in the morning. Here is a ticket for a flight on Tuesday and a return flight for Wednesday. A driver will meet you at the airport, and we'll take it from there."

Harry pulls a package of airline tickets from his vest pocket and hands them to Tim.

"Well, this is quite sudden, but I am committed to this ride, so to speak."

"Excellent. I'll see you in Chicago on Tuesday."

"This afternoon, I will give Howie Carr a call. I hope to set the record straight, and avoid an outbreak of street violence."

The two men stand up and shake hands. Harry turns and leaves and heads back to Le Meridien Hotel.

Harry arrives back at Le Meridien. As usual, an unmarked police car is parked with a view of the front entrance. Harry goes inside and to the front desk.

"Yes sir how we can assist you."

"I'm Harry Sharpstone, in room 334. Please have room service put together some sandwiches, hot coffee and cold beverages and serve them to the police cruiser parked across the street."

The desk clerk smiles and says, "very good Mr. Sharpstone. I'll have that done right away."

Harry decides to check in on Melio. He heads up to Melio's room, and knocks on the door. Melio answers the door.

"Oh, hi Harry, come on in. What's up?"

"How are you doing, Melio?"

"As a matter of fact Harry, I'm feeling much better. I plan to check out tomorrow."

"Melio, you can stay here for the weekend, but the mess has been cleaned up at your place, so you can head home whenever you want."

"Thank you, Harry, you have really done right by me."

"Melio, we take care of our union members. I'm glad we could help out. Now, I am heading back to Chicago in the morning. I'll be back in mid-June for the cab fare meetings with the City of Boston, and subsequent rate-splitting negotiations with the cab companies. Attorney Tim Martin has been selected for the new position of Boston Region executive for the union. I'm confident in his ability to do the job."

"I'm on board with that, Harry."

"Tim will oversee the local union steward meetings and general membership meetings. However, he will be relying heavily on working with the stewards to understand what is going on within each company."

"I've got it, Harry."

"One more thing. Two known thugs were shot execution-style last night in the North End.

"The word is that they were suspects in your assault. Melio, tensions are going to be running high. Please be careful."

"Harry, I have no idea who was shooting at me. I really have no idea."

"I know, Melio. I know. But, that's the way it came across on the news. I don't know how they made this connection to you on this shooting news story, but they did. So do not hesitate to call the police if you sense that you are in danger. Then call me, and then Tim. We are not tough guys, and we do not try to handle these situations ourselves. Got it?"

"Got it Harry."

"I'm going to try to get on the radio with that guy Howie Carr, and try to put out our position and defuse this situation. Now, tomorrow I have an early flight, so let's shake hands now, and I'll see you in June."

The two men shake hands, and Harry heads back to his room.

3:00 P.M. Harry turns on the radio in his room.

"Good afternoon, this is 'The Howie Carr Show', and I am Howie Carr."

Harry grabs his phone and calls in right away. He gets through.

"Hello, this is 'The Howie Carr Show', what topic do you want to discuss?"

"Hi, this is Harry Sharpstone with the Teamsters Union. I was hoping to address the rising tensions between the cab drivers and apparently the cab owners."

"Please hold, Mr. Sharpstone, I will put your call up first."

Suddenly Harry is hearing the radio broadcast through his phone.

"… .Earlier today it was reported that two thugs took two in the hat in the North End last night. Somehow they have been linked to the taxicab bombing and shooting in Charlestown earlier this week. Harry Sharpstone from the teamsters was nice enough to call in to offer his understanding on this story. Harry, are you there?"

"Yes Howie, hi. I appreciate this chance to make comment."

"Harry, lets here your statement on this, and then I 'll have a couple of questions. Go ahead."

"Thank you Howie. I spoke with the targeted cab driver about a half hour ago. He has no idea who pulled this off. We have no idea if these two executed men were in fact involved with the cab bombing. In addition, I want to emphasize that we do not condone any acts of violence. I call on all cab drivers to remain calm and professional. We have achieved union organization. We will be negotiating on the cab rates and ownership splits in June. Resolve for the frustrations of the cab drivers will happen soon, at these meetings."

"Mr. Sharpstone, my experience has been that unions over inflate wages, leading to higher fares and fees and less profitability for business owners."

"You can call me Harry. I cannot speak to all union circumstances, but the situation here is that cab drivers work sixty to eighty hours a week as self-employed independent contractors. That means that they are not guaranteed an hourly wage, and cab drivers in Boston typically earn five hundred to six hundred dollars per week. They receive no health insurance, vacation or holiday pay. In addition, the opportunity for them to move into cab ownership is almost impossible. The medallion for a taxicab in Boston is valued at about two hundred seventy-five thousand dollars. A handful of people own all of the medallions in Boston…

"There is a great imbalance between the earnings of the owners and the hard-working cab drivers. I'm hoping to achieve a realistic balance between these parties. I am confident that the balance achieved in the upcoming negotiations will inspire Boston's cab drivers to a higher level of energy, professionalism and satisfaction with their chosen line of work. The result may be that cab customers may get more service and professionalism for their dollar."

"Harry, that was a great explanation. I have to confess. I have just been enlightened about the plight of the cab drivers. I am shocked at the high value of taxi medallions. I had no idea. Why are they valued so high?"

"Howie, in Boston, the Chief of Police is in charge of the sale and oversight of taxi medallions."

"That sounds strange, Harry."

"It is strange, Howie. This is the only major city in the country that works this way."

"Why is that, Harry?"

"Well, as I understand, it comes under the heading of 'public safety' and that defers their oversight to the Chief of Police. In most other cities, it falls under the jurisdiction of the city transportation office."

"Somebody's found a revenue stream here."

"No comment, Howie. Look, this entire union organization process has been done as straight-forward and legal as possible. I strongly instruct the membership to continue to act properly and professionally. Let's keep this on the high road. I want to emphasize that the union and its membership is not behind any violent or covert acts. Let's all deflate this tension, and move forward as professional businessmen."

"Well stated, Mr. Sharpstone. Thank you for calling in and setting the record straight. I am certainly curious about this medallion process. Good luck going forward, and keep us informed."

"Thank you, Howie."

Harry hangs up the phone and takes a deep breath. He hopes that his message came across. He starts to pack up for the trip back to Chicago in the morning.

XIV

Tuesday, April 24, 12:00 Noon

Attorney Timothy Martin arrives in Chicago for his meeting with Teamster President James Hoffa. Tim is met at the airport by a cab driver. He is taken to the Wildfire Restaurant. Inside the restaurant, Tim is lead to a table in a private area. The two men at the table stand up to greet Tim. They are Harry, and Teamster President James Hoffa. The President carries the conversation.

"Tim, we were just about to order lunch."

Tim picks up a menu and makes a choice. A waiter comes by and takes their order.

President Hoffa begins, "Thank you very much for meeting with us today. I'm going to get right to it. Then we can enjoy our meal and the rest of the day. It is important that I continually groom people for upper leadership positions here at the national level. Presently, there are three managers who perform Harry's function nationwide. All three are in their mid to late fifties. With continued expansion, and the three current managers approaching retirement age, I plan to hire another manager within the next year. Harry speaks very highly of you, and has recommended you for just such a position. Tim, are you interested in continuing with the Boston assignment for about a year to a year-and-a-half, and then coming out here for a full-time position as a national manager for the Teamsters? This will require you to be a full-time employee. You will have to close down your practice to take this position. Before you answer, here is the starting pay and benefits package."

President Hoffa hands Tim a folder. Tim opens it up and reviews the numbers. Tim closes the file after a one minute review and replies, "Gentlemen, I am all in."

"That's great Tim. We look forward to having you on board. Our success as a labor union relies heavily on maintaining strong political connections, particularly those of a liberal Democrat persuasion for the most part. They are most supportive of our cause, and they seem to keep our perspective in mind when acting on legislation and formulating public policy. Therefore, I suggest that you make every effort to establish working relationships with liberal-minded politicians, both locally and nationally. We also like to retain strong ties with other unions such as the AFL-CIO, and the teachers union. When we are all of one voice on an issue, lawmakers listen."

"Thank you for that advice, Mr. Hoffa."

"Tim, please call me Jim."

The three men finish their lunch. As they stand up Harry says, "Tim, I'll be back in Boston on June 19th for the negotiations. In the meantime, keep me updated on any new issues. Oh yes, and keep an eye open for someone who can fill your shoes in Boston."

"Thanks Harry, I'll be sure to do that. As a matter of fact, there is a young man that comes to mind to fill the Boston position."

"Who would that be?"

"His name is Jay Mahoney. He has been driving a cab for seven years while attending classes at night. He has already completed his MBA, and this spring he graduated from Suffolk Law School."

"He sounds like a great candidate for the position. You can approach him as you see fit on this matter. I would like to meet him in June. We can make him an offer at that time, if you are still confident in him as a candidate for the position."

"Thanks Harry. I'll be sure to work on that. And thank you, President Hoffa. (Tim just could not bring himself to call James Hoffa, "Jim"). This has truly been a career advancement day for me. I am confident that I will meet your expectations."

Hoffa replies, "I'm sure you will Tim. I'm sure you will."

The three men shake hands. As Tim heads off to his waiting cab, he is thinking that life is good.

Tuesday, June 19th, 1:00 P.M.

Harry Sharpstone arrives in Boston for the Cab fare rate-setting meeting with the Mayor and the subsequent negotiations with the cab company ownerships. Harry sees Melio waiting for him at the baggage carousel inside Logan Airport. Both men smile. They greet each other with a hearty handshake. They have been through a lot together and have formed a strong bond.

Today, they embark on the final step to solidifying this union organization. This week, it is time to demonstrate the value of forming this union, as they will represent the united front of the cab drivers union in this all-important round of negotiations for a better life for the union membership.

Harry and Melio grab Harry's luggage and head to the cab. Harry stops and looks at Melio's new cab as Melio loads the trunk. Harry smiles, shakes his head and remarks "Wow, from the looks of this new cab, maybe it was time for the old one to get fire bombed." The two men laugh and jump in the cab.

"Where are we going boss?"

"I'm staying at the Park Plaza this time, Melio. Image is important when negotiating. You want to convey the strongest of positions to your opponent. The Park Plaza conveys that image. Everything must convey the right image. You must have the right power suits, ties, shoes, shoe polish, and haircut. 'It's 'Show Time', Ladies and Gentlemen.'

"I have a meeting with Attorney Tim Martin at two-thirty at his office. Why don't we go there first and take care of the business review for tomorrow's meeting? I'll check in later.

"Melio, I want you to sit in on this meeting. Your perspective will be helpful in knowing what it will take to satisfy the membership, and knowing what the membership is willing to give up in order to achieve their goals."

"Sure thing Harry," Melio replies. Meanwhile, he's thinking, "what is Harry talking about?"

They arrive at Attorney Martin's office on time. They proceed right in, and close the door. Tim has another person in the office with him.

"Harry, I would like you to meet Attorney Jay Mahoney. Jay, this is Harry Sharpstone."

Harry remarks, "Congratulations Jay, for recently graduating from Law School and passing the bar exam. That is certainly a lot to accomplish while driving a cab full time. I have heard a lot of positive things about you, and I look to working with you."

Jay responds, "Thank you, Harry. I appreciate the confidence you have in me, and I will deliver."

Tim finishes, "I'm sure that all of you have met Melio before."

The men exchange greetings, and sit down around a conference table.

Harry starts the meeting.

"Gentlemen, we are the negotiating team for the Boston chapter of the Teamsters Cab Drivers Union. Now, this year, Tim and I will do the talking. I am relying on you, Jay, to be a careful observer. Watch for telling body language. Note any strategies that you might see being played out, and when we go into a break, inform me of what you have seen. This will be very helpful to us, and it will also be a good preparation as we prepare you to be a primary negotiator for next year's session.

"Melio, you are going to be there as the eyes and ears of the rank-and-file membership. I will be looking to you for your reaction, as we are asked to concede something in order to get something. Now just what those 'somethings' might be, remains to be seen. I suspect that the Mayor will be looking for a commitment on our part to sharpen-up our level of professionalism in the cab industry, and to provide only clean and well-maintained cabs. He sees the cab drivers as ambassadors of Boston to those who are visiting from all over the world. He will want us to deliver a positive image of the city. We as leaders will have to instill this in our membership in order to achieve the rate increase that we will be plying for.

"In this round of negotiations, the cab owners will be our ally, because the drivers and the owners want to achieve the same result. We want to achieve the highest rate increase possible that the public is willing to accept. The Mayor's office will be looking to hold the line on behalf of the public's interest to save money. That is the frame of the issue for this first negotiation.

"Then Monday, assuming we have completed negotiations with the city, we will start negotiating individually with the owners of the cab companies."

"Ah, Harry," Attorney Martin jumps in. "If I may jump in here… "

"Go right ahead, Tim."

"Thanks. An attorney who represents the cab owners called me Friday, and said that the cab owners would like meet with us as one collective entity."

"Really?" exclaims Harry. "I need to think about that. You see, while it is convenient and efficient to reach a single agreement with the owners as a single entity, we may be able to drive a harder negotiation by dealing with them separately. We can put one against the other…

"If their competitor is offering its drivers a better deal, then they may steal away good drivers from their competitor. We may want to keep them off balance by not letting them to know what their competitor is doing.

"We have a week to make a decision on this. Let's think about this for a few days. Let's evaluate their demeanor at the Mayor's rate-setting negotiation. OK, what are the details on the rates?"

Tim passes out a set of printed pages to the group, and informs them, "OK, currently the city has established maximum rates as follows: Two dollars, forty cents for the initial fare charge, two dollars forty cents per mile, and two dollars per minute for idle time. We need to achieve two sixty-five for the initial fare charge, two sixty-five per mile and two-twenty per minute for idle time. If we maintain a fifty-fifty split with the owners, these rates will create a five percent pay increase to the drivers, and an additional five percent to pay their union dues. Anything above that level is gravy. Therefore, I propose we start the negotiation by asking for three dollars for the initial fare, two-eighty per mile and two-fifty per minute for idle time."

Harry sounds off, "I like it Tim. Good job. What do you two gentlemen think?"

Melio responds, "I had no idea how this kind of thing works, but it all sounds pretty good to me."

"Jay, how does this strategy sound to you?"

"Well, Harry the rate negotiation strategy looks very sound. I think we can exceed our minimum acceptable level. But where does the union's contribution for the group's health insurance program come from?"

"Good question Jay," responds Harry.

"Fifty per cent of the monies received as dues from the membership is applied directly toward supplementing the health insurance premium. This should actually cover about ten to twelve percent of the premium for a single individual. If these negotiations go as planned, cab drivers will finally have group health insurance available to them through the union at about ninety percent of the cost of an individual policy."

"That sounds good Harry." Jay responds. "I'm ready for tomorrow."

"Great, now we all know our role in this proceeding. So let's plan to be at the conference table at 10:00 A.M. ready to go."

The meeting breaks up. Melio takes Harry to the Park Plaza Hotel, where he checks in and winds down for the day.

Cab Fare Rates

Current	Minimum Acceptable	Asking
Base:		
$2.40	$2.65	$3.00
Per mile:		
$2.40	$2.65	$2.80
Per minute:		
$2.00	$2.20	$2.50

Wednesday morning 9:55 A.M. Harry and Melio walk into the conference room at the Mayor's office in City Hall. Tim and Jay are already present.

The negotiating team for the cab owners, walk in and take their place at the table. The Mayor's negotiators walk in, sit down, and call the meeting to order.

"Ladies and Gentlemen, this meeting is called to order. Now we all know what the current rates are for cab fares. I request that you hand me your submission for proposed rate changes at this time."

Attorneys for the union and the cab owners hand their proposals to the meeting chair. The Mayors negotiators quickly review their submissions and prepare to respond.

"Folks, the Mayors Office believes that the rates submitted by you are all too high. We are prepared to make a strong suggestion for new rates to be adopted. While it is not the rate levels that you want to see, we believe it represents a reasonable increase that will not touch off objection from the general public. We have put a lot of thought into these proposed rates and we strongly urge you to support their adoption.

"We propose a base rate of two dollars seventy cents, with a rate of two dollars and seventy cents per mile and an idle rate of two twenty-five. Can we get your support for these rates?"

Tim and Harry realize that these rates exceed their goals on all levels. They exchange a glance and Harry nods. Harry speaks up. "In the spirit of cooperation and harmony, the drivers union is in agreement with your proposed rate schedule."

The cab owners group has gone into a bit of a huddle at their end of the table. They break their huddle. Their spokesman announces, "The coalition of cab owners find this rate schedule to be acceptable."

The meeting mediator takes over. "Since all parties are agreed on the new rate schedule, I declare this meeting adjourned."

Harry whispers to his group. "Don't say anything until we get outside and back to Tim's office."

The group picks up their gear and heads out the door, down the elevator and regroups in Attorney Martin's office. The group is elated with what was just achieved.

Harry addresses the group. "Congratulations gentlemen. We just hit a home run. Sometimes these negotiations go just that easy. Let's not sell ourselves short, though. The strategy we laid out yesterday of what to ask for could have set the tone to achieve what was just achieved. Let's represent this as a meeting where the union achieved acceptance with the other parties involved, and the mediated result represents a step in the right direction for the cab industry and a reasonable fare structure for the general public."

Attorney Tim jumps in. "This is a tricky situation. Let's not be over-jubilant about this. That could come back to work against us next year. However, let's take a stand that the presence of the teamsters union undoubtedly made a positive difference in this negotiation process. Now, how do we want to handle negotiations with the cab owner's next week, Harry?"

"Suddenly, Tim's office phone rings.

"Hello."

"Hello Attorney Martin, this is Mayor Flynn."

"Well, hello, Mayor Flynn, my negotiation team is here with me in my office. Would it be appropriate to put this call on speaker phone?"

"That is a great idea. Thank you."

"How can I help you Mr. Mayor? The three other men in the room are paying close attention."

"First, I wanted to say thank you to you and your negotiation team that attended the meeting at my office this morning. Your team demonstrated professionalism and understanding, which certainly made the proceeding smooth and reasonable. I would also like to mention that my team intentionally made what I believe was a generous offer, in order to settle the matter immediately.

"Let's avoid a prolonged negotiation which could overshadow the arrival of the tall ships in Boston on Saturday morning."

"I see." Tim responds. "Is there anything else?"

"Well, yes. Since the city will be full of tourists and sailors on leave from Saturday through Thursday, there will be a very high economic surge for the city during that time period. It is highly beneficial for all of us to be working harmoniously during this critical time of high economic activity. I am hoping that in light of the generous offer made by the city this morning, the cab owners and cab drivers now have the leeway in their earnings to reach an equally expeditious conclusion to the remaining negotiation. I really hope that this matter can be wrapped up by the end of the day on Friday."

"I see," Tim responds. "Well, Mr. Mayor, I will certainly keep your position on the table as we proceed. It is the hope of all of us that a reasonable agreement be reached swiftly."

"I have relayed the same message to the cab owners coalition, and urged them to call you today to get this process in motion," Mayor Flynn responds. "Likewise, I urge you to take the first step today and achieve a successful resolve."

"Thank you, Mr. Mayor. Your message is received and noted, and I will contact the cab owners' counsel shortly if they have not tried to contact me."

"Very good, Attorney Martin. Have a good day."

The group absorbs the Mayor's message.

"OK," Harry starts off, "first of all, Melio please order some pizzas to be delivered for lunch. We are probably going to be here a while."

"Our goal is to achieve the best result possible. Achieving the highest possible cab fare rate along with the largest possible share of that cab fare rate is the dominant goal. However, we must be careful not to push beyond the tolerance of the public, the Mayor, and the cab owners. Creating negative relationships could cost the membership market acceptance and encourage people to look for alternatives to us. Let's keep that in mind.

"Now, the cab owners sense an opportunity for higher revenues based on the increased fare rates. Frankly, that is reasonable. However, I want to change the structure of how the drivers share revenue with the cab owners. Presently, they simply charge the drivers rent for the cabs. This puts all the risk of the marketplace on the drivers. The owners don't' care if we make fares or not, because they get their cab rent. Presently, the cab rent averages out to about fifty two percent of the fares received.

"My proposal is that we simply split all fares fifty-fifty. This formula means the more fares earned, the more the cab owners earn as well. The drivers will make more money by virtue of the increased rate, and take on less risk because when business is slow, their pay out for the cab is low."

"I've got it Harry." Tim replies. "Shall I call them now and see how it goes?"

"Go ahead… " all of a sudden Tim's Phone rings.

"Hello Attorney Martin, this is Attorney D'Angelo. I represent the Cab owners coalition. Is this a good time to talk?"

"Please hold for just a minute, Attorney D'Angelo," Tim responds.

He puts Attorney D"Angelo on hold. Then he addresses his group.

"Gentlemen, the timing could not be better. This is Attorney D'Angelo on the phone. He represents the cab owners' coalition. I'll put him on speaker-phone. Harry, I will work off your hand signal for direction. But I recommend that the conversation be just lead counsel to lead counsel."

"OK, Tim." Harry responds. "Let's do this. We can always pause and take it under advisement and get back to him if need be. Agreed?"

The other three men answer in unison, "Agreed."

Tim puts attorney D'Angelo on speaker-phone, and begins to speak. "Attorney D'Angelo, thank you for holding. I have you on speaker-phone. As luck would have it, the cab driver's negotiation team is still here in the office with me. They are Harry Sharpstone from the Teamsters National office, Attorney Jay Mahoney, and Melio Rocco. Is this OK with you?"

"Absolutely, Attorney Martin. Let me begin by saying that the cab owners coalition found your group reasonable to do business with, and in the spirit of being reasonable, they have asked me to extend an offer on behalf of their entire group that makes complete sense for this initial year of this business relationship.

"We estimate that new rate structure will increase cab fares by about twelve percent. Therefore, we propose a ten percent increase in cab rental fees. This leaves positive gains for the drivers, and an ideal rent increase for the cab owners."

"I see, Attorney D'Angelo." Tim responds. "That proposal is certainly close to ideal. However, I wish to propose a structure that provides similar yield to all parties, while shoring up a cooperative partnership, so to speak, between the owners and the drivers. I propose a simple fifty-fifty split between the drivers and the owners. What do you think?"

"Well, let me put you on hold for a minute so I can talk it over with the group."

"OK, we'll hold."

Two minutes later the conversation resumes. "Tim," Attorney D'Angelo begins, "Well, I do not have a consensus on your proposal. I propose that we all break for lunch and discuss the proposal on the floor. Then, I'll give you a call back at two o'clock and see where we stand."

"That's a great idea, Attorney D'Angelo. I'll expect your call at two o'clock."

The pizzas arrive. The group pauses for lunch Harry pipes up, "My guess is that owner Ragatini is the holdout. His kid is the one that blew up Barry and put a beating on me. I'm sure he has a chip on his shoulder."

Tim speaks up. "Harry, you want to be careful with Ragatini. The word is that he rules the North End Mob. His connections run all the way back to the Patriarca family in Providence."

"Now, Tim, I'm not afraid of Ragatini or Patriarca. The Teamsters have done business occasionally with the Patriarca family. I just might have a connection or two there, myself."

Harry's cell phone rings.

"Hello?"

"Well hello, Mr. Sharpstone."

"Hello, Senator Bulger. What can I do for you today?"

"I understand that you are actively negotiating with the cab owners. Mayor Flynn just called me and asked if I could expedite a resolve to an apparent point of contention. Can I be of any help?"

"Thank you for offering, Senator Bulger. I believe we have the matter under control."

"That's excellent, Mr. Sharpstone. I told the Mayor that we can count on you to put this process to rest. Have a good afternoon."

"Thank you, Senator Bulger. Your message is received. Have a good afternoon."

At 2:00 sharp, Attorney Martin's phone rings.

"Hello, Tim, it's Attorney D'Angelo."

"Hello, Attorney D'Angelo. What's the good word?"

"Well, Tim, despite some political pressure to get this done, I do not have a consensus of agreement from the cab owners. The owners are holding out, and are not willing to change to a fifty-fifty split structure. Their position is that this would leave their revenue stream reliant on the ability of the drivers to maximize their ability to do business. Conversely, simply charging rent for the cabs solidifies their revenue stream, and removes the marketplace variable from them."

"Well, Attorney D'Angelo," Tim replies, "The cab drivers believe that the fifty-fifty split provides an incentive for the owners to provide top-notch cabs. Top-notch cabs will make them more appealing to the customer base, creating more desire to use them, and maybe even greater tips of appreciation."

"Tim, I understand your perspective, and I will convey it to the owners, but I don't see them budging. I'm gonna tell ya, the holdouts were not happy. I'm gonna need some time to speak to the group and get a response. Let's plan on speaking again tomorrow at one o'clock."

"That will be good," Tim responds. "I'll review this with my clients and we will talk tomorrow."

"Well guys, you heard him." Tim remarks. "Harry, where do we go from here?"

"Tim, we're not going anywhere. You've presented our position and reasoning very well. I say we stand on this position. Let's all meet here at twelve forty-five tomorrow, and see how this hand plays out."

"Harry, if I may," Jay Mahoney jumps in. "We have already achieved all that the drivers could hope for, and I sense a heightened level of friction and resistance as we push for this one last concession. Conversely, leaving this last bone of contention on the table and meeting them in agreement will alleviate pressures of the opponents at this stage, and will establish a better negotiating relationship going forward. Meanwhile, we have already exceeded our expectations. I recommend that we take all that we have won and seal the deal."

"Harry, I have to say, I agree with Jay," says Tim.

"Melio, what do you think?" asks Harry.

"Well, Harry, I agree with the two attorneys. We have already won here. It might be a good idea just to wrap it up."

Harry pauses. He actually agrees with the group, but this is his way of sending a message to the owner who's son delivered the beating to him, that he is not intimidated or wavering.

"OK, we've already called it a day." Harry responds, "So let's just wait until the meeting at the One O'clock call tomorrow, and if they do not concede then we will, and we'll wrap it up."

Harry and Melio head out and take a ride over to Charlestown, where the U.S.S. Constitution is docked.

The U.S.S. Constitution is the World's oldest commissioned naval vessel. It has three masts and is two hundred four feet in length overall. It was named by President George Washington, launched in 1797, and was one of six original frigates authorized for construction by the Naval Act of 1794.

The scene at the pier is one of preparations for the tall ships event. Spectator ropes are being set up. The crew aboard the Constitution is busy in preparation. This will be a big event.

There will be over one hundred tall-mast sailing ships on parade in Boston Harbor on Saturday Morning. This will be a great spectacle to kick off the summer season in Boston, and about one hundred thousand spectators are anticipated from all over New England, the country and the world. The atmosphere in the city is high-spirited. It will be a great time for the spectators, the sailors, the merchants, and the city.

Next they head over to the North End. Harry and Melio take a stroll along Hanover Street. Hanover Street is the site of many feasts and street festivals throughout the summer months. The smells of Italian dishes fill the senses. The sounds of rock, popular and cultural music fill the air. It is a happy and relaxing place to escape on a summer evening. Tonight, preparations continue for the Tall ships event.

"Thanks Melio," Harry says. "I needed to clear my head. Just feeling the vibration of anticipation of the tall ships weekend has restored me to my senses. Tomorrow, we will wrap this up and move forward. In retrospect, you and I have accomplished a lot here, my friend. You are truly a good friend, and a quality guy."

"OK Harry. Don't get all mushy on me. Jeees! Let's get out of here and call it a day."

Melio takes Harry back to the Hotel. On the way back to the hotel the chatter on the two-way radio has an air of heightened tension over the unresolved negotiation.

Thursday, 10:45 A.M

Harry's cell phone rings.

"Hi Harry, It's Jim Hoffa. How are things going there?"

"Good Jim, I should wrap things up here this afternoon, and be on my way home tomorrow. Is something wrong?"

"Well, the Mayor of Boston called me this morning, and ripped into me. He claims we are grandstanding and he was not too happy."

"Jim, I have this under control, and it will all be wrapped by two P.M today."

"That's great Harry. I'll see you when you get back."

"Thanks for calling Jim."

Harry has never had a call from Hoffa like this. He senses that he might have pushed a little too hard this time, but this will all be wrapped up in three hours. Besides, his mission is to get the best deal possible for the Union members. That is all he is doing.

Harry puts on the radio.

"This is Listo Fisher with the news at 11:00. Tensions are running high over the cab fare rate negotiations. Cab drivers have started to talk about a strike. Meanwhile, Boston prepares the arrival of over one hundred thousand visitors this weekend with the arrival of the Tall Ships. The Mayor assures us that this will be resolved in short order and there will be no cab strike... .."

Harry turns off the radio. Once again, he realizes that he may have pushed too hard this time. He gets cleaned up and gets dressed for the meeting.

Melio picks up Harry at 12:00 noon and they head off to Tim Martin's office. They walk in at 12:45. Tim and Jay Mahoney are already in the office.

"Good afternoon gentlemen." Harry starts in. "OK, let's listen to their position, and if they are not willing to concede then let's make the concession and get this deal done. Oh yea, Attorney Mahoney, I'm a little distracted today. However, I must say that you have done a fine job. I would like to discuss retaining your legal services for the Boston Chapter and other business, but not today. We'll talk sometime very soon."

"Thank you, Mr. Sharpstone," Attorney Mahoney responds. "I look forward to our discussion."

Just then the office phone rings.

"Hello, It's Attorney D'Angelo here."

"Hello, Attorney D'Angelo, it's Tim Martin and I'm Here with Attorney Mahoney, Harry Sharpstone and Melio Rocco."

"Gentlemen, let me get right to it. A lot of pressure has been applied to my clients to get this done. The final owner was very reluctant to go along with this, but finally conceded at the urging of all of the other cab owners to get the deal done. The cab owners have agreed to the fifty-fifty split."

"That's great. So we have a deal?"

"Tim, we have a deal. I'll take care of packaging up this resulting agreement, as well as the agreement from the earlier meeting yesterday, and get it over to your office for signatures in just a few days. Thank you, Tim, Mr. Sharpstone, Attorney Mahoney, and Mr. Rocco, and I'll be in touch."

The four men are elated at what has been accomplished. They have completed what could have been a difficult six- to eight-day negotiation ordeal, in just two days. In so doing, they have also accomplished and achieved everything and even more than they had set out to accomplish.

Harry stands up. "Tim I suppose you can handle the remaining paper work."

"I certainly can, Harry."

"Superb. In that case, our work here is done. Carry on. Melio, can I have a ride back to the hotel?"

Melio takes Harry back to the Park Plaza. While on the way back to the hotel, Harry makes a call and changes his flight reservation for tomorrow at 2:30 P.M.

"Melio, I want you to be sure to get the word out on the result of today's negotiations."

"Harry, I just can't wait to tell the boys."

"Great, and don't forget to pick me up at noon tomorrow. I have a two-thirty flight to Chicago."

"OK, Boss."

Harry approaches the hotel front desk.

"Yes sir, what can I do for you?"

"I just wanted to let you know that I'll be checking out at 12:00 Noon tomorrow, and I wish to check for messages."

"Sir, you have no phone messages. However, there is a very attractive woman named Margaret Patriarca waiting for you in the cocktail lounge."

Harry pauses, shakes his head and smiles. Then he strolls into the hotel cocktail lounge. He walks up to the bar and sits down next to a well-dressed slender woman. She has long straight brunette hair and dark brown eyes.

"Hello, Margaret, it's nice to see you."

"Well, hello there, Harry."

"What brings you to town?" Harry asks.

"My black Mercedes Benz coupe brought me to town. It brought me to town because I heard you were here in Boston, and I miss you. When you said good bye on April 12th I had no idea that you would be gone so long, so I decided to come see you."

"I see. And how did you find me, my dear."

"Harry, my last name is Patriarca. I can find out whatever I need to know… my dear. Now, please sit down and have a drink with me and a bite to eat."

The two have drinks and then dinner. They catch up on their lives events and share some laughs.

Then Margaret says, "Harry, I'm not driving back to Newport, Rhode Island tonight. Can I stay here with you?"

Suddenly, the gruff yet cool Harry Sharpstone is tense and confused. He takes a deep swallow, slowly collects himself, and answers. "OK."

Then he calls over the bartender, hands him her valet parking ticket and says, "Ms. Patriarca will be staying this evening. Please have her luggage delivered to my room."

The bartender responds. "Very good, Mr. Sharpstone, right away."

Harry grabs the bottle of Champagne from the ice bucket, and the couple proceeds up to Harry's room.

Raymond Patriarca, Margaret's uncle, renowned Rhode Island mobster and New England crime family boss, controlled most of the Italian Mafia operations in Boston, the North End and points north, including Charlestown. The mafia was notorious for providing protection to business owners, for a fee.

It is suspected that Raymond Patriarca's client list includes the cab owners of Charlestown and the North End.

Harry and Margaret were introduced by Uncle Raymond two years ago. They have maintained a clandestine relationship ever since. One might not know if Uncle Raymond would approve of this relationship, and one might not want to risk finding out.

XVII

Harry and Margaret are at the front desk checking out. Harry addresses the desk clerk.

"These charges look fine. Please charge this to my credit card. Thank you very much. Please have Ms. Patriarca's car brought around to the front door."

"Very good sir, and thank you for staying with us at the Park Plaza Hotel."

The two make their way through the front door. There is a group of news reporters out front waiting to confront Harry. Harry and Margaret look into each other's eyes, smile, hug and part ways. Margaret walks toward her waiting car and Harry approaches the reporters.

"OK guys, let me give you a statement. I'm sure that this morning's news covered the details of the agreement achieved yesterday. I want to commend the Mayors office, the Cab owner's coalition and the people of Boston for accepting and working with the newly formed cab drivers union of Boston. The agreements achieved yesterday demonstrate that these groups can reach a working agreement, satisfactory to all, cordially and professionally. Thank you."

Melio slid over and grabbed Harry's luggage during the press speech. The two move off toward Melio's cab and get in. They set out for the airport. They head for the Callahan Tunnel, which takes downtown traffic directly to the airport. The mid-day news is just ending on the radio.

"… I'm Listo Fisher. Now it's time for 'The Howie Carr Show'." Howie opens his show.

"Thank you, Listo. I must say, I have been covering the city scene here in Boston for many years, and this cab driver's union negotiation seems to be missing something."

"What do you mean Howie?" asks Listo.

"Well, Listo, it appears to me that the cab owners have had the muscle of the Mafia in the North End working for them. The bombing of Barry Blumberg's car, the tire slashing episode, the beating of Harry Sharpstone, and the bombing of Melio Rocco's cab all have the fingerprint of the North End Mob, and we all know that Raymond Patriarca runs that show."

Suddenly, Harry perks up and listens intently. Could Margaret actually be in town to keep an eye on him for Uncle Raymond?

The cab turns into the tunnel. Traffic is moving slowly. There are only two lanes of traffic in the tunnel. There is a ramp truck in front of the cab, and its emergency lights are on. There must be a breakdown ahead in the tunnel. Just then traffic comes to a complete stop.

… "What do you mean, Howie?" asks Listo. "What do you expect might happen?"

"Well Listo, Raymond Patriarca is capable of any dreadful act. For example, when Raymond Patriarca wants to take care of business, one of his signature moves is to have a car cornered. Then his boys open fire on the car, shooting its occupants beyond recognition. He usually has a ramp truck waiting to pick up the bullet-ridden car and haul it away. Rumor is that they take the cars down to the pier, where a waiting cement mixer fills the car with concrete. Then they load the car onto a waiting barge and take it out into the vast sea. Finally, the car is dumped into the sea, leaving its deceased occupants to spend eternity swimming with fishes."

Traffic starts to move through the tunnel as if nothing has happened. The radio is still playing in the cab.

"I'm Howie Carr."